*Books by Frank Fields*
*in the Linford Western Library:*

MOUNTAIN CITY
MAIL ORDER BRIDE
THE BLOODING OF JETHRO
THE MARSHAL AND THE
DEVIL MAN
RIDING SHOTGUN TO DENVER
MUD CITY MURDERS
HUNT FOR GOLD

KT-381-551

# GREENWOOD VENDETTA

Billy Nesbitt is released from prison after serving thirty years for a crime he did not commit, and he sets out to exact retribution on the man really responsible. However, his target, James Fairfax, a landowner in Greenwood, is expecting Billy and tries to prevent him ever reaching the town. Billy's quest becomes a battle between his desire for revenge and his conscience. He has some difficult choices to make and questions to answer — but can he survive long enough to see justice done?

DM

013597949X

**SPECIAL MESSAGE TO READERS**

This book is published under the auspices of

**THE ULVERSCROFT FOUNDATION**

(registered charity No. 264873 UK)

Established in 1972 to provide funds for research, diagnosis and treatment of eye diseases. Examples of contributions made are: —

A Children's Assessment Unit at Moorfield's Hospital, London.

•

Twin operating theatres at the Western Ophthalmic Hospital, London.

•

A Chair of Ophthalmology at the Royal Australian College of Ophthalmologists.

•

The Ulverscroft Children's Eye Unit at the Great Ormond Street Hospital For Sick Children, London.

You can help further the work of the Foundation by making a donation or leaving a legacy. Every contribution, no matter how small, is received with gratitude. Please write for details to:

**THE ULVERSCROFT FOUNDATION,**
**The Green, Bradgate Road, Anstey,**
**Leicester LE7 7FU, England.**
**Telephone: (0116) 236 4325**

**In Australia write to:**
**THE ULVERSCROFT FOUNDATION,**
**c/o The Royal Australian and New Zealand**
**College of Ophthalmologists,**
**94-98, Chalmers Street, Surry Hills,**
**N.S.W. 2010, Australia**

FRANK FIELDS

# GREENWOOD VENDETTA

WARWICKSHIRE
COUNTY LIBRARY

CONTROL No.

*Complete and Unabridged*

# LINFORD
*Leicester*

First published in Great Britain in 2004 by
Robert Hale Limited
London

First Linford Edition
published 2005
by arrangement with
Robert Hale Limited
London

The moral right of the author
has been asserted

Copyright © 2004 by Frank Fields
All rights reserved

British Library CIP Data

Fields, Frank
    Greenwood vendetta.—Large print ed.—
Linford western library
    1. Western stories
    2. Large type books
    I. Title
    823.9′14 [F]

    ISBN 1–84395–876–7

Published by
F. A. Thorpe (Publishing)
Anstey, Leicestershire

Set by Words & Graphics Ltd.
Anstey, Leicestershire
Printed and bound in Great Britain by
T. J. International Ltd., Padstow, Cornwall

This book is printed on acid-free paper

# 1

James Fairfax read the telegraph that his lawyer pushed across the desk, sat in silence for a few moments and then sighed deeply.

'So they're letting him out in two weeks' time,' said Fairfax. 'I was kind of hoping that he might have died in prison.'

'Well he didn't,' said the lawyer. 'I don't know what it is between you and this Billy Nesbitt and I don't think I really want to know. It must have something to do with the murders of your father and brother, but that was a long time ago.'

'Thirty years,' said Fairfax. 'He murdered my father and my brother, Carl. Had he been older — he was only sixteen — they would probably have hanged him. They don't hang sixteen-year-olds though. Instead they

1

gave him thirty years.'

'It was a long time ago,' said the lawyer. 'Why are you so interested in him now?'

'Just a feeling,' relied Fairfax. 'You're probably right. I don't think he'll come back here. There's nothing for him to come back to.'

'You don't really believe that,' said the lawyer. 'I can tell from the way you are talking. Even if he does come back what can he do to you? I think there's something you're not telling me. Don't go doing anything stupid.'

'I won't,' nodded Fairfax. 'How far away is the prison?'

'Sonora,' said the lawyer, 'best part of five hundred miles.'

★   ★   ★

Billy Nesbitt jumped slightly as the large doors slammed shut behind him. For a short time he stared unseeingly ahead before turning to look at the large doors of the prison. That building

2

had been his home for the past thirty years, the only home he had ever known apart from his first sixteen years. Even the memory of those times of his youth were, for the most part, now very distant, almost as though it was something that had happened to someone else. However, certain things were as fresh in his mind as if they had happened only yesterday.

Few people in the small community which surrounded the prison even bothered to look at him as he glanced around. Prisoners being released were a common enough sight and most soon moved on, only too anxious to get as far away as possible. Billy had seen the community many times during his thirty years and he had even been through the town of Sonora, some five miles away. On those occasions though, he had always been in a chain gang, a working party sent out to carry out seemingly useless work. The only good thing that had come out of these otherwise mindless tasks were that he now had a powerful muscular body.

In that respect he had been more fortunate than most other prisoners. At first his age, sixteen years old when committed, had been in his favour and he had learned very quickly that the only way to survive was to do exactly as he was told. There was no doubt about it: he, Billy Nesbitt, had been a model prisoner. Some of the older guards even appeared genuinely sad to see him go.

Now, quite suddenly and even quite brutally in a way, he was free to do as he pleased, go where he pleased when he pleased. The only trouble was that he was not at all certain if he was pleased. All he had in his pockets were ten dollars given to him by the chief warder and a slip of paper with a name and an address. He did not know the address, he had never learned to read. All the guard on the gate had said when he had opened the door was that the man named would find him work if he wanted. He was not at all certain if he wanted work, but he did need more money.

Billy picked up the small canvas bag that contained his world. A rather blunt folding knife, a spoon and fork, a worn and very faded pair of long johns, a shirt and the only thing of any value he possessed, a gold locket containing the now faded and chipped miniature painting of a young woman — his mother.

Apart from these few possessions, Billy had been given a new pair of denims, a denim jacket, new boots, a hat, a shirt and new underwear. He had remarked that it was not much after such a long time in prison. The governor had pointed out that he was one of the lucky ones — most long-term prisoners did not survive their sentence. Billy questioned who were really the lucky ones.

The only skill Billy had acquired during his imprisonment was the ability to fight. One of the few activities allowed to the prisoners, and even actively encouraged by the guards, was bare-knuckle fighting. Many wagers had been won on his ability to beat the living daylights out of almost any man.

'The Sonora Timber Company,' the owner of a nearby store informed Billy when he asked what the note said. 'Just let you out, have they?' Billy nodded, staring round at the myriad of things he could not remember ever seeing before. 'How long?' continued the storekeeper. Billy looked blankly at him. 'How long have you been in?' asked the man again.

'Oh, sorry, sir,' said Billy. 'Thirty years. At least that's what they tell me.'

'Thirty years!' said the storekeeper with a slight whistle. 'What you do, murder somebody?'

'Yes, sir,' said Billy, 'Two people actually.' The storekeeper stepped back slightly, obviously startled. 'At least they tell me I murdered them. I don't remember much about it. I was only sixteen.' That was a lie. Billy remembered every minute detail as though it had only just happened.

'Where you headed for?' asked the storekeeper.

Billy thought for a few moments before replying. 'Don't rightly know, sir,' he said. He automatically called everyone 'sir', it was something he had had to do for the past thirty years. 'I thought maybe I'd head back to Greenwood. That's where I was born.'

'Can't say I know the place,' said the storekeeper. 'Got family there, have you?'

'I don't think so,' said Billy. 'My ma an' pa died a long time ago. I used to have an uncle there, but I reckon he's probably dead as well by now.'

'Take my advice,' said the storekeeper. 'If you've got nothin' to go back for, forget it. The chances are you probably won't be welcome there anyhow.'

'I reckon you're right about that, sir,' said Billy. 'In fact I'm damned sure I wouldn't be welcome. I do have some unfinished business there though.'

'Any business you had was finished

thirty years ago,' advised the store-keeper. 'It don't do no good to rake over old feuds and grievances. I'd say your unfinished business is more to do with revenge than anythin' else.'

'Revenge?' said Billy. 'No, sir, it ain't got nothin' to do with revenge. More to do with justice.'

'Same thing,' said the storekeeper. 'Now, can I get you anythin'?'

'No, I don't think so,' said Billy. 'I've only got me ten dollars. Where is this timber company? I was told they would probably find me some work. Right now I need to earn me some money.'

'Four miles, straight up the main road,' said the storekeeper, pointing. 'Just before you reach Sonora. The man you want is Mike Gittins. Watch out for him, he's real mean taskmaster.'

'Can't be no meaner than them in there,' said Billy, nodding in the direction of the prison. 'I reckon I can deal with anythin' he cares to throw my way.'

Billy left the store and wandered

along the street, stopping briefly outside a building which proclaimed itself to be the 'Last Chance saloon'. For a few moments he toyed with the idea of going inside. He had never been inside a saloon in his life. In fact he had never tasted beer or whiskey in his life. Strangely though, he had no particular desire to correct that oversight.

A woman came out, plainly not dressed for the street, something which even Billy with his lack of experience could see.

'Just let you out have they?' she said, giving him a broad smile. 'What you need is a woman. Come on inside, I'll show you a good time. Only five dollars.'

Billy felt himself blushing. 'Thank you, ma'am,' he mumbled. 'I have me some business to attend. Maybe some other time.' He did not want to admit that he had never had a woman. In fact he had never seen a naked woman.

'Suit yourself,' she pouted, turning sharply and disappearing.

Billy abandoned the idea of going into the saloon and continued his walk towards Sonora and the timber mill.

'Sure, I was told you might be along,' said Mike Gittins at the mill. 'I hear you've been in there for the past thirty years. That's one hell of a long time. I hear some good reports about you though. About how you is a good worker and in particular about how you is one hell of a fist fighter.'

'Is bein' a fist fighter a good thing?' queried Billy. 'All I'm interested in is earning some money. I need to get to a place called Greenwood, but I need to buy me a few things before I do.'

'If you're as good with your fists as they say you are,' said Gittins, 'you can earn your money a lot faster'n I can pay you. OK, you're hired. Pay is a dollar a day plus a bed in the bunk house an' two meals a day. You get every Sunday off, but apart from that you work from six in the mornin' until six at night. Pay day is every other Saturday. Any questions?'

10

'When do I fight?' asked Billy. 'You said I can earn good money fist fightin' an' since I need money fast, when do I fight?'

'Most Sundays,' said Gittins. 'I pay you one tenth of all the money I win on you. Sometimes that can be ten dollars a fight or even more, for yourself.'

'Half,' said Billy. 'I get half of all you make. If I lose, we both lose. The thing is, I don't lose.'

'Half!' exclaimed Gittins. 'No deal. You start off with one tenth. You win me some money an' I'll think about increasin' your share. First though, you got to prove yourself. I've already got a tough one lined up for you for a start. Curly Kabbanitch. He's usually called Curly to his face on account of he ain't got a hair on his head. Behind his back folk call him The Cabbage but he don't like that. If you want to get him real riled, you just call him *Cabbage*.'

'Does he work for you?'

'No, he works for Matt Parker out at the Big Pine Timber Mill, couple of miles the other side of town. Been with Matt a couple of months now, ain't lost a fight yet.'

'OK, Mr Gittins,' agreed Billy. 'You're on. I fight this time for one tenth. After that, we talk about it. Now, when do I start work?'

'Too late for today,' said Gittins. 'I'll get my foreman to show you where you bunk an' eat. He'll assign you work in the mornin'.'

'Is there much call for fighters round here?' asked Billy.

'Sure is,' said Gittins. 'This town was built on timber and most of the men round here don't know any other way of life except fightin' and humpin' timber. You're a big feller, you should fit in well if what I hear is only half right.'

'Can't say as I want to spend my life luggin' timber an' fightin',' said Billy. 'Still, right now I need me some money.'

'Just do as you're told an' I'll see to it that you get your share,' said Gittins.

Even with his lack of experience in

the wider world, Billy felt that he was being used, a means to an end and that if he started to lose a few fights, he would be discarded. He had seen similar things happen in prison. For the moment, however, he felt that he had little choice in the matter.

The food in the camp, although plain, was far better than anything he had ever eaten in prison and the bunk he had been allocated more comfortable than the thin palliasse and hard boards he had slept on for the past thirty years. In fact he found the comparative comfort made for uneasy sleeping at first.

The following morning he was assigned the task of loading sawn timber boards on to railroad wagons, which would then be transported throughout the country. For the next two days Billy worked the only way he knew how — hard.

Saturday night was the one night when almost everyone deserted the camp for the delights the town of

Sonora had to offer. Billy was persuaded to go along with a couple of men he had been working with. For the first time in his life Billy entered a saloon. He found it noisier and dirtier than he had expected and at first the smoky atmosphere made him choke.

'New face,' said the bartender. 'Gettin' to be quite a thing round here. You're the third new face in three days. Work for Mike Gittins, do you?'

'It's a livin',' said Billy, looking round at everyone, most of whom appeared intent on pouring as much beer or whiskey down their throats as they could. 'How much is your beer?'

'Twenty-five cents a glass,' said the bartender. 'Whiskey an' rum is fifty cents a slug. We don't have no champagne.'

'Champagne!' said Billy. 'What the hell's that?'

'That's why we don't sell it,' said the bartender with a dry laugh. 'Nobody knows what it is.'

'I'll try a beer,' said Billy, not wanting

to appear different from the others. He dug into his pocket and pulled out a coin. 'Twenty-five cents. I can't read so I don't know what this is, but it looks like it's enough. I reckon I'll have to teach myself to read sometime. Although maybe at my time of life it's too late. I'd better learn numbers though.'

'Now that tells me one thing,' said the bartender. 'You must've spent a long time down at the prison.'

'Thirty years,' said Billy without thinking.

'Thirty years!' whistled the bartender. 'That also explains why you said you'll try a beer. That kind of thing deserves some sort of celebration. This one's on the house.' He handed Billy a glass of beer. Billy took the glass, sipped at it and grimaced slightly, but after a second sip decided that it did not taste so bad.

The two men he had come in with had disappeared and although he recognized a few faces, nobody seemed anxious to be seen with him. Even in the camp most of the other workers had shied away from him on learning that he had spent thirty years in prison for murder. However, Billy was not too concerned. He rather enjoyed his own company.

A woman approached him, offering him a *good time* for five dollars. As before, Billy felt himself blushing and refused the offer. It was not so much because never having been with a woman he was frightened by the prospect, but more to do with handing over five dollars for the privilege. At that moment he was intent on accumulating enough money to be able to buy himself a horse, a saddle and possibly a gun. The woman simply smiled and moved on to another man.

A short time later, two men approached him, one of them offering to buy him another beer. Billy did not refuse, it meant another twenty-five cents saved.

'You must be Billy Nesbitt,' said one

of the men. 'I'm Matt Parker, owner of the Big Pine Timber Company. I hear you are to fight my boy Curly Kabbanitch tomorrow.'

'So I've been told, Mr Parker,' said Billy.

'Curly is one hell of a fighter,' said the other man. 'In fact he's just about the best we've ever had. We've been hearin' some good things about you as well. In fact most of the prison guards have bet money on you an' they ain't known for throwin' their money away.'

'I've been told I'm good,' admitted Billy, 'but I don't have anythin' to judge against. I never found a prisoner I couldn't beat though.'

'I also hear you're only interested in makin' money,' said Parker. 'I'll go along with that, what man in his right mind isn't. The thing is, Billy . . . you don't mind if I call you Billy, do you?' Billy shook his head. 'Good, I can see you an' me is goin' to get along just fine. The thing is, we'd hate to see Curly lose. We've got too much money

17

ridin' on him. Know what I mean?'

Billy looked at both men for a moment. He knew exactly what Parker meant. He had been ordered to lose fights in prison on more than one occasion, but he had always refused. At first that refusal had cost him dearly in bad treatment and food even worse than usual. Even so, he had continued to refuse to throw a fight and in the end most guards and certainly all the other prisoners had respected him for it.

'Are you askin' me to go down?' asked Billy.,

'You learn fast, Billy,' said Parker with a broad smile. 'You throw this fight and I'll see to it you don't lose out on the deal. How does fifty dollars sound?'

'Fifty dollars sounds great,' said Billy. 'Only problem is, I don't know how to lose. I only ever fight one way an' that's to win. Sure, I know that one day I might come up against a man who beats the daylights out of me, but that's fair. I don't mind losin' fair. I just don't know how to lose deliberate. Who knows, maybe your man is the man to beat me.'

'I'm a powerful man around Sonora,' said Parker. 'If I want somethin', not even men like Mike Gittins can stop me. Let me put it this way, Billy: this time you lose the fight. I've got too much money ridin' on Curly Kabbanitch to risk that he can beat you fair and square. If you beat him, I'll see to it that both your hands are crippled so bad you'll never be able to fight again. Do I make myself clear? You lose an' I'll pay you fifty dollars. How much is Gittins payin' you? If I know him, he won't pay a penny more'n he has to an' I'll take bets it ain't fifty dollars.'

'I'll think about it,' said Billy. It was the thought of fifty dollars which made him waver, not the threats. 'Thanks for the beer, Mr Parker.' He raised his glass and moved away.

'I see you talkin' to Matt Parker,' said the bartender. 'I hear you're fightin' Curly Kabbanitch tomorrow. Seein' the way Matt was talkin' to you, maybe

I should have me a few dollars on Curly.'

Billy suddenly decided what he must do. 'I reckon a few dollars on me might be a better bet,' he said. 'I don't throw a fight an' I sure don't give way to threats, no matter who makes 'em or why.'

The bartender studied Billy for a few moments and then nodded his head. 'OK, if you say so, I'll risk me ten dollars on you. Now, maybe I'll be doin' you a favour. See them two men over at the table in the corner by the window . . . ?' Billy glanced across and nodded. 'Well they've been askin' about for you. I ain't got the faintest idea who they are or what they want, but I've been in this business long enough to smell trouble when I see it. You are Billy Nesbitt, ain't you?' Billy nodded. 'The thing is, they know your name as well an' they've never set foot in Sonora before as far as I know. They're the two strangers I mentioned. Take my advice an' steer clear of them two, at least until after the fight.'

'Thinkin' about your ten dollars?' said Billy with a wry smile.

'That an' your health,' said the bartender. 'You're a big feller right enough an' a sane man would never take you on his own, but remember that you've been inside for thirty years. That means you don't have any experience of the wide world or the men who live in it. I tell you, them two is lookin' for trouble.'

'Trouble I can give them,' said Billy. 'OK, so I don't have what you call experience of the world, but unless you've been in prison you have no idea just what a dog-eat-dog life is like. I can look after myself.'

'Just a warnin',' said the bartender.

Billy leaned on the counter and studied the two men in the corner for some time. They were not particularly big men and in a fist fight he had no doubts that he could take on both at the same time and hardly lose breath. However, the guns at their sides told him that even he could not stop a bullet.

His first visit to a saloon had so far proved rather disappointing. He had heard of dancing girls and other stage shows, but there was none of that in this particular saloon. Its purpose appeared threefold: to sell beer, whiskey and rum, take as much money off the timber workers as possible at the gaming tables and then for scantily clad women to take what they had left.

His first taste of beer had been something of a disappointment in that he had expected something stronger, but it was otherwise acceptable. Gambling had been a common form of relaxation in the prison, but he had never been tempted by it and, until now, he had never had the opportunity to take a woman. Of the three, he thought he preferred the beer. It was cheap enough to be affordable on occasion whereas the other two pleasures were very expensive. There was a chance of making a profit by gambling, but he knew full well that such a thing was not for the inexperienced.

Having had enough, he decided to go back to camp. He had been tempted to ask what the two men wanted of him, but decided that they would let him know when they were ready. It was about a mile back to the camp and being a Saturday night, the roads in and out of Sonora were deserted.

He was about halfway back when he suddenly became aware of two figures behind him heading in the same direction. It was too dark to make out who they were, but somehow he did not think that they were fellow workers returning to camp. He decided that the best way to find out would be to wait for them. There was a bend in the road which temporarily hid him from view. He took the opportunity to hide amongst the bushes that lined the roadside.

The two men had apparently quickened their pace when he had disappeared from view and, when they rounded the bend, suddenly stopped. Billy heard one of them swear.

'Lookin' for somebody?' asked Billy, stepping out of the bushes, close to one of them.

The man's reaction was to turn slightly and attempt to draw his gun. Billy's reaction was slightly quicker and his fist slammed into the man's face before the gun had left the holster. The second man also attempted to draw his gun, but once again Billy's fist was quicker and this time slammed into the man's chest. Both men fell to the ground as if they had been poleaxed. Billy stood over them, almost challenging them to do something. They both wheezed and grunted, the one wiping blood from his face. They looked up at Billy and even in the faint moonlight, Billy could see the fear in their eyes.

'I figured it might be you two,' said Billy, his fists still clenched tight and threatening. 'I heard you was askin' about me. I don't know what it is you want, but you might've got the answer you needed if you'd bothered to ask me.'

'We don't know what you're talkin' about,' said the man who had been hit in the chest. 'We was just takin' a walk, that's all. Ain't no law against a man takin' a walk is there?'

'Not as far as I know,' said Billy. 'Why were you askin' about me back in the saloon?'

The two men glanced at each other, neither attempting to get up. 'I . . . we heard you were due to fight Curly Kabbanitch tomorrow,' said the man with the sore face. 'We're both gamblin' men an' we just wanted to know which way the fight was likely to go.'

'You're not the first,' said Billy. 'Even Mr Parker wanted to know that. He ain't none the wiser either. I hope you don't mind if I say I don't believe you, gentlemen. For your information, my name is Billy Nesbitt and I have just served thirty years in prison for murderin' two men. It might've been a long time ago, but killin' somebody is somethin' you don't forget too easily, unless that's the kind of thing you two gentlemen do for a livin'. I've met all types in my time and survived them all. Now, I'll ask again. Why are you so interested in me?'

'We told you,' insisted the one. 'We just wanted to know where our money had the best chance on the fight tomorrow.'

'OK, have it your way,' said Billy. 'I guess I'll find out the real reason soon enough. All I can say is that Mr Parker made it plain that I had to lose the fight. He even said he'd pay me fifty dollars if I did. Now, gentlemen, I'm goin' back to the Sonora Timber Company camp. If I so much as get a smell of either of you followin' me, I can assure you my fists are just as capable of killin' as your bullets. Do I make myself clear?'

The two men, muttered that he made himself perfectly clear, struggled to their feet and then ran off back to town.

# 2

Sunday morning: Billy was given a bigger and better breakfast than usual and then taken on a wagon to the venue where the fight was to take place. As well as Billy, there were three other fighters, two of them quite small men. The third, roughly the same height as Billy, was not as well built. He soon discovered that he and Curly Kabbanitch were the main attraction, the others merely supporting roles. Billy did wonder if he should tell Mike Gittins about the approach by Matt Parker, but he decided against it.

The site for the fight was in a natural amphitheatre and already it seemed that the entire population of Sonora and the surrounding districts had taken their places on the side of the circular bowl. Billy saw a few faces he recognized, guards from the prison, and all waved to him and indicated that he knock the hell out of his opponent. He also looked around for the two men he had encountered the previous night. He could not see them, but he had the feeling that they were there somewhere.

As he had expected, the other three fights were to take place before his and he was forced to wait patiently in the wagon at the top of the hill whilst his three travelling companions attempted to spread as much of their opponents' blood and brains as possible over the arena.

There was only one rule of bare-knuckle fighting and that was that there were no rules, apart from not being allowed to kick a man whilst he was on the ground. There were no rounds, no breaks other than breaking bones, and the fight started when the referee told them to start and only ended when one of the combatants was knocked unconscious or refused to get up when knocked down. It had been known for a fight to last an hour or more, but that was most unusual. Billy had found that most men gave up when it became obvious that they were not going to win.

Of the three fights prior to Billy's, the one which lasted the longest was between the two smallest and thinnest men. After about fifteen minutes the man from the Sonora Timber Company was declared the winner. The next fight, lasting about ten minutes, went to Matt Parker's man. The third fight, which lasted no more than five minutes, also went to the man from the Big Pine Timber Company. Now it was Billy's turn and to loud cheers and boos in more-or-less equal proportion, he was led, bare from the waist upwards, down into the arena.

The referee, who also acted as Master of Ceremonies, announced each fighter in turn, beginning with Curly Kabbanitch. He was hailed as the unbeaten heavyweight champion — of where it was never specified — with eight fights and eight wins under his belt. He strutted arrogantly around the circle, waving to the crowd and informing them that they were about to witness win number nine.

Billy was presented as a new fighter with an unproven track record. He was actually quite pleased when no reference to his time in prison was mentioned, although it was by that time common knowledge. In contrast to his opponent, Billy simply raised a hand to acknowledge the crowd.

'Just remember,' said the referee as he called the two men together, 'no kickin' a man when he's down. That apart, you can do what the hell you like. Now let's see a good fight an' may the best man win.'

'You will not last two minutes,' sneered Kabbanitch. 'I am from Russia and all Russians have eaten bigger men than you before breakfast.'

'I don't eat people,' responded Billy. 'Russians give me wind, they make me fart. Most are like you, all wind and no fight.'

The referee pushed them apart, raised his hand and suddenly lowered it to his side. Both men raised their fists and for a few moments moved around, each looking for an opening.

Kabbanitch was the first to strike, but Billy had been expecting it and easily dodged the blow. At the same time his punch landed hard into Kabbanitch's stomach. This obviously came as something of a surprise to the Russian, although it did not appear to hurt him too much.

'That was a lucky punch,' hissed Kabbanitch. 'That was all the luck you will get. Prepare to die, *murderer*.'

Once again Kabbanitch lashed out but the blow simply glanced off Billy's head. Billy's return blow was right on target, crashing into the Russian's face. He reeled backwards, blood streaming from the corner of his mouth. There was a gasp from the crowd, most of them sensing an upset to what they had considered to be a forgone conclusion.

Even after such a short time, Billy

was beginning to get the measure of the Russian. Kabbanitch obviously knew of only one way to fight and that was to hit hard and hope. Billy on the other hand had learned how to move, how to ride punches and when to strike. Once again the Russian faced him squarely. This time it was Billy who struck first.

His blow tore through Kabbanitch's weak defence and landed hard on his face. This time blood flowed from the Russian's nose. However, although surprised at the way things were going, he was far from beaten. Suddenly they were in a clinch.

'It seems your Mr Parker doesn't have much faith in you,' whispered Billy. 'He says he'll pay me to lose this fight.'

'I do not need you to throw it,' hissed Kabbanitch. 'I win because I am the better fighter.'

'Prove it, *Cabbage*,' challenged Billy.

The answer surprised Billy this time. From seemingly nowhere, the Russian's fist slammed into his face and it was all he could do to prevent himself falling to the ground. He felt blood running down his face, from where he had no idea, and did not attempt to find out.

Although Kabbanitch was not a fighter with much finesse, he was nevertheless a very hard man to put down. Billy made him stagger a few times but he refused to go down. For about ten minutes they traded blows, Billy generally getting the better of the exchanges. However, being the better mover did not count. The only thing that mattered was putting your opponent on the ground and making him stay there.

By that time both their faces were covered in blood and blood was seeping into Billy's eyes, making it difficult for him to see. Once again they were in a clinch, both using the opportunity to take a breather, much to the annoyance of the crowd.

'You have enemies,' hissed Kabbanitch into Billy's ear. 'I have been told I will receive one hundred dollars if I kill you. I have killed men before.'

'So have I, remember,' responded Billy.

A heavy blow landed in Billy's stomach and he very nearly went down, but he managed to hold on. A second blow landed in his face and this time he could not prevent sinking to his knees. This brought loud cheers from the supporters of Kabbanitch and the referee pushed the Russian to one side. Billy struggled to his feet, temporarily blinded by blood in his eyes. Kabbanitch rushed forward, apparently sensing that Billy was finished.

Billy was even beginning to think that the Russian was unbeatable, but as Kabbanitch closed in, Billy, still blinded, lashed out. He heard a gasp from the crowd, followed by a brief silence and then cheering from a small section. He wiped the blood from his eyes and saw the Russian lying on the ground.

Kabbanitch was completely motionless, his face now almost unrecognizable as such beneath the blood and livid flesh. The referee bent over the body, studied it for a few moments and, since there was no sign of life, went over to Billy and raised his arm, declaring him to be the winner. Loud cheers erupted from those who had wagered on Billy and boos from those who had lost their money.

'Well done!' enthused Mike Gittins, rushing over to Billy but stopping short of hugging him. 'I knew you could do it.'

'I was beginning to wonder,' gasped Billy. 'That was the hardest fight I've ever had. How is he?'

'Who cares,' laughed Gittins. 'You won, that's all that matters. You just earned yourself twenty dollars.'

'Not bad,' gasped Billy, still trying to catch his breath. 'A couple more fights an' I'll have enough to get to Greenwood.'

'So what's at Greenwood?' asked Gittins. 'You've got a great future here.'

'I don't think Mr Parker will agree

with you,' said Billy. 'He told me I had to lose the fight. He was goin' to pay me fifty dollars if I did. I reckon you can afford to pay me fifty for winning.'

'Think yourself lucky I'm payin' you twenty,' said Gittins. 'Maybe next time, if I think you're worth it. I'm goin' to arrange a re-match against Kabbanitch.'

'So what about Mr Parker's threat to see that my hands were crippled if I won?' asked Billy. 'I won't be much use to anybody if that happens.'

Gittins simply shrugged. 'That kind of thing is normal business,' he said. 'I try to bribe and threaten his boys an' he does the same to mine. Sometimes it works, sometimes it doesn't.'

By that time the body of Curly Kabbanitch was being roughly man-handled up the slope. Billy followed, rather concerned about the Russian. He was so lifeless he feared that he might have killed him. He reached him just as he was literally thrown on to a flat wagon.

'How is he?' he asked of Matt Parker.

'How is he?' sneered Parker. 'It's only too right that you should be worried. I told you to lose the fight. I don't take it kindly when somebody ignores my orders.'

'I don't know what happened,' said Billy. 'I'll admit it, I was almost beaten. When he came at me I thought that was the end. He would have won fair.'

'But he didn't,' muttered Parker. 'Maybe you didn't see it, but that last punch of yours nearly took his head off. Your days as a fighter are numbered, *Mr Nesbitt*. You'll be hearing from me when you least expect it.'

'Thanks for the warning,' said Billy. 'It won't be unexpected now, will it?'

Billy was taken back to the camp with jubilant supporters either side where, much to his surprise, he was examined by a doctor. The doctor declared him badly bruised but otherwise uninjured. He was allowed a bath — in itself a most unusual occurrence — and allowed to rest on his bunk. It did not take long before he was soundly asleep.

*   *   *

Winning the fight did not mean that Billy was allowed to take it easy. His muscles still ached and his face was still very sore, but the following morning he was expected to carry on his normal work.

During the morning Mike Gittins came to him and handed him the twenty dollars he had promised, with the warning that it did not entitle him to get drunk and miss work. Billy had no intention of getting drunk or spending his hard-earned cash in any way other than to purchase what he needed to get to Greenwood.

For two days Billy continued to load railroad wagons and it was during that time that he began to take an interest in where each wagon was destined for. He was unable to read, but he managed to find a pencil and piece of paper and painstakingly copied what he was told was the destination. This was chalked on a black piece of board attached to each wagon. Eventually he had six possible place names.

His idea was to hitch a ride on a wagon he knew would be going in the general direction of Greenwood. The only problem he encountered was that nobody seemed to have the faintest idea where Greenwood was.

It was one of his bunkhouse companions, one of the few who would talk to him, even after his win, who suggested that he talk to Father Sean Ryan, the local priest. He was assured that if anyone knew where anywhere was, Father Ryan was sure to know.

'Ah yes, pleased to meet you at last,' greeted the priest when Billy presented himself later that evening. 'I liked the look of you as soon as I first clapped eyes on you. I said to myself, now there's a man who knows how to fight. I was right too. I won ten dollars on you. You handled yourself just like some good old Irish fighters. Now they were real fighters. You're not Irish, are you, by any chance?'

'Don't think so, Father,' said Billy. 'I was born in a place called Greenwood, but I don't think it was in anywhere called Irish.'

Father Ryan laughed. '*Ireland*,' he corrected, 'Not *Irish*. Ireland is way across the sea near a place called *England* — may God forgive me for using such foul language. So, you were born in this country. That's fair enough, we can't all choose where to be born. Billy Nesbitt,' he mused. 'Are you sure your parents weren't Irish? I once knew a Michael Nesbitt from County Mayo, but he did have some Scottish blood in him. At least he wasn't cursed with English blood.'

'I think my mother came from somewhere called Bavaria, but I don't know where that is. My pa and his pa were born an' bred in Greenwood.'

'Bavaria,' said the priest. 'They're Germans there I believe. Even that's

40

better than bein' cursed with English blood.' He laughed. 'You will have gathered by now that I am not over-fond of the English. I hear you've just been released from prison after thirty years. That's a long time in anybody's language. I take Mass once a month at the prison. Did you ever attend? I certainly don't remember you.'

'I'm not a religious man,' confessed Billy. 'My ma used to go to church sometimes, but me an' my pa never went. I don't know what religion she was an' religion sure didn't play a big part in prison life.'

'Unfortunately,' said the priest. 'So, if you're not a religious man, what brings you to me?'

'I want to get to Greenwood,' said Billy. 'Nobody seems to have heard of it though. I was told you were the most likely person to know where it was.'

'Greenwood,' mused the priest. 'Offhand I can think of three Greenwoods. One is in New York State, one is in

Texas and the other is about five hundred miles north-west of here. There's sure to be more I don't know about as well. Take your pick.'

'It was a long time ago,' said Billy, 'but when I was brought here, I think it took about a week travellin' in a prison wagon.'

'Then my guess is that your Greenwood is the one about five hundred miles north-west of here.'

'Do you know if there's a railroad link from here to there?'

'Now that I *do* know for certain,' said the priest. 'I'm afraid the answer is no. From here the railroad goes south to a place called Toledo and north to Warren Junction. From Warren Junction there's another line which runs east–west. That's how it got the name Warren Junction on account of the two railroads cross there. Now if you were to ask me the nearest place to this Greenwood, I'd say go to Warren Junction an' take the line which heads west. Mind, I'm only guessing. If you intend going, they should be able to tell you where Greenwood is at Warren Junction.'

'I have some names here,' said Billy. 'I can't read or write, but I copied them from boards on the railroad trucks I'm loadin'. Do they mean anythin'?'

The priest studied Billy's unsteady scrawl and smiled. 'All I can tell you is these two places are south of here, these two are definitely a long way north, much further than your Greenwood and these two I don't really know, but I'm guessing north. The point is, all those heading north have to go through Warren Junction.'

'Then I guess north it is,' said Billy. 'Thanks for your trouble, Father. How far away is Warren Junction?'

'About forty miles. Good luck to you,' said the priest. 'I do believe that like me, you are a man with a mission, but that mission has been interrupted. Take care, do not do anything stupid. Perhaps one day I shall return to Ireland to continue with my mission for

43

an Ireland free of English rule.'

Billy's mind was now set. He had thirty dollars and would have more come Saturday pay day. It was a lot less than he had set his mind on, but it was enough to last until he reached Greenwood. He was always prepared to work for a few dollars or even his keep. He might never be able to afford a horse and saddle or a gun, but he was not afraid to work or walk. Although he was anxious to reach Greenwood as soon as possible, he was wise enough to realize that a few more weeks was not very long to wait after thirty years of waiting.

★　★　★

The following morning Billy, along with others, was assigned work in the forest, assisting the tree fellers or lumberjacks as some of them preferred to be called. Their job was to trim all the unwanted branches from the trees, pile them up and set fire to them. All he had to do was make sure that the fire did not spread. It was emphasized that keeping the fires under control was a very responsible job. If the forest burned down, they were all out of work. Nevertheless it was hardly taxing work, but the knowledge that he would be away on the first available train load of timber to head north after Saturday made the work seem almost enjoyable.

Billy was staring into the flames, leaning on a stick and allowing his mind to wander. Up until that point the one thing that had been at the forefront of his mind had been nothing more than the determination to get back to Greenwood. Exactly what he was going to do once he got there had never really come into it. Now, however, on the verge of his thirty-year dream becoming a reality, he did begin to think of what he would do and how he would do it. The name *James Fairfax* seemed to occupy his every thought.

Suddenly, he became aware of someone calling. He looked about but there was nobody to be seen. There it was again and this time he was convinced it was his name being called. Once again he looked about and there was another call. On this occasion he managed to locate the direction from where it came.

'Yoh!' he called in the manner of most of the tree fellers. 'Yoh! What you want?'

'That you, Billy?' came a distant call. 'I need help, I got myself stuck.'

'Keep callin',' shouted Billy. 'I'll find you.'

Five minutes later he came across a man from his bunkhouse apparently trapped under a large, heavy branch.

'Damn thing rolled down on top of me,' said the man. 'I can't move. I think I might've busted my leg.'

Billy attempted to pull the man out, but his cries of pain made him stop. He looked at the thick branch and tried to lift and push it away, but it was either too heavy or it was lodged somewhere.

'Try liftin' that end,' said the man,

indicating the narrower end of the branch. 'I reckon it's got itself stuck in a hole or somethin'. If you move it, I think I can get myself out.'

Billy moved the ten feet or so to the end of the branch, managed to get a grip and was about to lift when he heard a loud cracking noise and a sudden movement caught his eyes. He looked up just in time to see a huge tree falling straight down on him.

★ ★ ★

'He's under there somewhere,' said one of the lumberjacks to two men. 'I'd say he's dead all right. No man could survive that size of tree fallin' on him.'

'I'd like to see the body first,' said one of the two men. They were the two men Billy had encountered on the road back from the saloon. 'No body, no money. That was the deal.'

'Hell, man,' complained the lumber-jack. 'It's goin' to take a hell of a long

47

time gettin' through that lot. Thing is, even if he ain't dead yet, he's sure to be badly injured an' if we leave him he'll die sure enough. It gets mighty cold out here at night at this time of year.'

'No body, no money,' insisted the man. 'I reckon your boss will want to see the body anyhow so you might as well dig him out. Don't worry, we'll be around for a couple of days yet. You bring us proof he's dead, you'll get your hundred dollars an' not before.'

'OK, OK,' grumbled the lumberjack. 'I'll go tell Mr Gittins. You just make sure you're still in town tomorrow. Come on Greg,' he said to the man who had appeared to be trapped. 'If we take our time gettin' back, it'll be dark, too dark to start lookin'. Don't you worry none, gents,' he said to the two men. 'By the time we get to him, he'll be dead even if my axe accidentally slices the top of his head off.'

★   ★   ★

Billy recognized the voices, particularly that of the lumberjack. If he was right, it was another man from his bunkhouse, a man by the name of Ginger McCoyle. The man who had lured him into the trap was Greg. That was the only name Billy knew him by, but he knew the face well.

Somehow, when the tree had fallen, Billy had managed to avoid the main trunk and had landed in a shallow hollow. The hollow was just deep enough to take his body but he was surrounded by a tangle of branches. He had been about to call out when he had heard the men talking and realized that if he had let it be known that he was still alive, he would most certainly be killed. He briefly asked himself why the two strangers wanted him dead, but such thoughts quickly gave way to the matter of freeing himself.

It was not easy; a large, thick branch lay across his chest, pinning him down. Apart from a few obvious cuts and bruises, he did not appear to be hurt and he did not think there were any broken bones.

He tried pulling himself, using the branch as a lever, but his head hit a large rock and it was obvious that he could not free himself that way. Next he attempted to slide under the branch, but soon found himself firmly wedged. He rested for a few minutes thinking about what to do and eventually came to the conclusion that the only chance he had would be to somehow raise the branch to allow him to slide out.

This was easier said than done, but after many attempts to raise the branch, he suddenly felt the pressure on his chest ease slightly. Once again he summoned all his strength and, sweating profusely, felt the branch give a little more. It was just enough to enable him to slide downwards and eventually the branch was free of his chest but resting on his neck. His problem now was that he had moved too far to allow him to get a grip on the branch and lift it again. Once again he rested, gathering his breath.

The ground beneath his head seemed quite soft and he managed to get one hand up towards his head. He then spent quite some time trying to remove soft earth from beneath his head. It took what seemed an eternity, but he eventually found that he had just enough room to slide his head under the branch.

Suddenly he was free, even if there was still a tangle of smaller branches and leaves over him. He rested for a while before struggling to find a way out. Once he was free, he did not show himself immediately, just in case anyone was still around. He slowly pushed his head through the leaves and looked about.

It was now quite dark and, apart from a few bird calls, there was no sign of life. He slowly eased himself out and clambered over the tangle of small branches. He crouched by the side of the fallen tree, looking and listening.

Once again his thoughts returned to the question why the two strangers were so anxious to see him dead.

He decided that there was only one way to find out. He had to confront the strangers. He also decided that Ginger McCoyle and Greg needed to know, in no uncertain manner, that he was still very much alive. For the moment though, he thought it better if all concerned believed that he was still beneath the tree.

# 3

Locating the two strangers proved a lot easier than Billy had expected. He saw them entering the first of the three saloons in Sonora. Having discovered where they were, Billy was content to sit in the shadows opposite the saloon and wait. He was very experienced at waiting.

Very few people used the side of the street where Billy was. There was no boardwalk and it was mainly occupied by whorehouses, whereas all the possible places of interest such as the saloons, eating house, stores, barbers and bathhouses, were on the opposite side. He was, however, joined by a black and white Jack Russell terrier whose one demand was that Billy scratch his head occasionally.

How long Billy waited for the two men to reappear, he did not really know and did not particularly care. He and the Jack Russell followed them along the main street, finally ending up outside a rooming house. They did not appear to be in any hurry and sat outside. Once he was satisfied that there was nobody about, Billy approached the men.

At first they plainly did not recognize Billy, but when they did, it was too late to run. Billy smiled as he towered over them.

'Surprised to see me, gentlemen?' he growled. The Jack Russell also growled at them.

'Surprised?' quavered one of them as they both stood up. 'Why should we be surprised. It's a free country.'

'That's what they've been tellin' me for the past thirty years,' said Billy. 'You know, that's an idea that still takes some gettin' used to. Somethin' tells me you know all about that. Now why should either of you want to kill me? Oh, don't bother to deny it. I was under that tree when you were talkin' to Ginger

McCoyle an' that man called Greg. One hundred dollars was the price if an' when they discovered my dead body.'

'Don't know what the hell you're talkin' about,' said one of them. 'We ain't never heard of nobody called Ginger McCoyle or Greg. Anyway, why the hell should we want to pay anybody to kill you? I can assure you that if we wanted you dead, we are more than capable of doin' it ourselves.'

'Probably you are,' agreed Billy. 'Only trouble with that is if it goes wrong you get into trouble. If somebody else bungles it, they take the blame.'

At that moment two other men stomped along the boardwalk, obviously the worse for drink. They saw the two strangers, but did not appear to notice Billy who had moved to one side and behind the men and was now in a shadow, his huge hands gripping the back of each man's neck.

'We told Mr Gittins Billy hadn't turned up an' that we thought he was trapped under a tree,' slurred Ginger McCoyle. 'We waited till it was dark. We said we'd never be able to find the tree in the dark. He's organizin' a search party for the mornin'. Just make sure you're around with our money.'

'You're drunk,' growled one of the men.

'Sure, we're drunk,' admitted Greg. 'Tonight we can afford it, tomorrow we'll be rich. C'mon, Ginger, I still got me a couple of dollars left, we're wastin' good drinkin' time.'

They staggered off, apparently still not noticing Billy behind the two men. Even so, Billy did not ease his grip on the men's necks.

'Seems they might've made a mistake too,' he sneered. 'Now, gentlemen, I need answers to a few questions.'

'Take your hands off our necks,' croaked one of them. 'Mine feels like it's goin' to snap at any moment.'

'And snap it will, if I don't like your answers, my friend,' warned Billy. 'Now why did you want to kill me? Mind, I reckon there's no need to answer that. I've been doin' me a bit of thinkin' an' I reckon I can answer the question myself. You must be workin' for James Fairfax from Greenwood. Am I right?' He squeezed their necks to reinforce his question. Both men attempted to nod. 'Good, I like that answer. I don't suppose he ever told you why he wanted me dead, that's somethin' he wouldn't want the whole world to know.'

'OK, OK,' gasped one of them, managing to break free of Billy's grip. 'We admit it, we were sent here to make sure you never reached Greenwood. We ain't done nothin' wrong yet though. The law can't touch us for a damned thing.'

'Perhaps the law can't touch you,' snarled Billy, 'but I can. First, I think I'll take that hundred dollars you were going to pay McCoyle and Greg. I think I'm letting you off lightly.'

'Go to hell!' grated the man still in Billy's grasp. 'We know you killed Mr

Fairfax's father and brother, that's good enough for us. You ought to have been hanged as well.'

'I didn't kill 'em,' snarled Billy, his grip tightening on the man's neck. 'He did, but I saw exactly what happened and he set me up. I've just served thirty years of my life in prison for that man. I intend to live long enough to see that he suffers for it.'

Although he had not realized it, Billy's grip had tightened to such an extent that the man's neck was in imminent danger of breaking. Had the man not tried to struggle free, Billy might well have eased his grip. As it was he attempted to pull Billy's hand away and at the same time break free.

There was an ominous crack, a slight choking sound from the man and he slowly sank to the ground. The other man stared in horror for a few seconds and then ran down the street. Billy seemed to realize exactly what he had done and was also about to make a run for it when a familiar voice close by spoke to him.

'Take my advice and stay precisely where you are, my boy,' said Father Sean Ryan. 'I saw exactly what happened. I was standing over there when Ginger McCoyle and his friend were with you. You know, I do believe they were so drunk they never even saw you. I know that what happened just now was an accident on your part, but I'm not so certain that the sheriff is going to look upon it quite so kindly, especially if you make a run for it.'

He came over and bent down by the dead man, partly to confirm that he was actually dead and then, rather surprisingly as far as Billy was concerned, to draw the man's gun which he then placed partly under the body, close to the man's hand.

'What are you doin'?' Billy asked.

'Makin' it look like self-defence,' said the priest. He searched the body, found a wad of money which he handed to Billy. 'Take this, you might be in need of it. Now when the sheriff arrives, you just act dumb an' let me do all the talkin'. I heard all that about them working for James Fairfax so I won't really be tellin' lies now, will I? Don't you worry none, young Billy, you'll be fine. Just trust me.'

Sheriff Eric Wells and one of his deputies arrived about ten minutes later, led by the other stranger. All three seemed very surprised to see Billy.

'Looks like you got some explainin' to do,' growled the sheriff. 'Just goes to prove what I always say, once a murderer always a murderer. Most seem to stay out of trouble rather longer'n you have though. Mr Wellings here was tellin' me that you were demandin' money from them and when they wouldn't pay, you killed him.'

'Now it wasn't really like that, Eric,' said Father Ryan. 'I saw exactly what happened and it was all in self-defence, and I am prepared to swear to that on the Holy Bible. I think you'll find a gun under the body somewhere. He tried to shoot young Billy here, only Billy was a bit too strong. I think his neck is broken.'

The sheriff looked at the other man, Wellings, whilst the deputy searched under the body, producing the gun.

'You didn't tell us about that,' said the sheriff. 'You claimed Nesbitt deliberately broke his neck.'

'The priest is lyin',' protested Wellings.

'And why should he do that?' asked the sheriff. 'I think some explanation might be in order down at my office. That includes you, Father, if you don't mind.'

'Or even if I do mind?' said the priest with a broad smile.

At the office, Father Ryan explained what he had witnessed and overheard. Billy confirmed everything the priest said and even Wellings conceded that they had been sent by James Fairfax to make certain that Billy never reached Greenwood. However, he still insisted that Billy had broken his companion's neck deliberately and that the gun was

61

never produced. Having Father Sean Ryan as a witness more than satisfied the sheriff and Billy was allowed to go free. He was not even searched for the money.

Outside the office, Billy tried to thank the priest but was told that the best thing he could do now would be to leave Sonora on the first available train north to Warren Junction. The priest seemed to think that a load of timber was leaving early the following morning. Once again, Billy thanked him and wandered back to the Sonora Timber Company camp. His new-found companion, the Jack Russell, trotted happily alongside him.

Being a Saturday night, the camp was deserted. Billy was owed money for the work he had done so far, but he was not over-anxious to follow that up. He now had plenty of money, far more than he ever thought he would have. During his few days at the camp, there had been one man who had spent some time with him, attempting to teach him numbers.

Billy thought that he might be able to find out how much money he did have from the little knowledge he had gained so far. He found an old piece of meat on one of the other bunks, gave it to the dog and then he placed all the money he had on his bunk.

At first, he placed two different notes he knew about, a ten dollar bill and a five dollar bill, on the bunk. He then sorted out all the other notes that were the same on top of these. This process took the majority of the money and left him with five notes which did not match either of them. Of these three were plainly the same and two were different. He carefully placed all his money into four piles, put the notes into his small leather bag and decided to go and ask Father Ryan how much he had. Once again, the dog kept him company.

'One hundred and fifty-seven dollars,' announced the priest. 'These two here, they're one dollar notes . . . ' Billy studied the notes carefully. 'Fives and tens you say you know. That's good. These other three are twenty dollars each.' Once again Billy picked up a note and studied it. To confirm that he had got the idea, he showed each one in turn to the priest and told him what it was. He was quite pleased when he was correct. 'Oh, by the way,' continued the priest, 'that man Wellings has been kept in jail on suspicion of conspiracy to murder or something. It'll be a hard charge to make stick, especially if you're not around. It will keep him out of circulation for a few days though. Nobody in town appears to have heard a thing about what happened, so you shouldn't have any bother from anyone.'

Billy once again thanked the priest and returned in the general direction of the camp. However, a short distance in front of him, obviously finding it very difficult to keep their balance and using each other as support, were his two bunkmates, Ginger McCoyle and Greg.

They were approaching the bridge

over the Sonora River and at that point the river passed through a deep, narrow gorge with a drop from the bridge of at least forty feet and there was no guard-rail. Billy eventually caught up with the pair in the middle of the bridge.

'Been havin' a good time?' Billy asked casually as he came up behind them. 'You can hardly stand.'

'Yes, thanks, Billy,' replied Ginger McCoyle without thinking. 'We got us a whole lot of money comin' tomorrow.' He suddenly stopped and stared at his companion for a short while. Greg stared back in disbelief. 'Billy!' Ginger managed to croak. 'That you, Billy?'

'No, I'm a ghost,' said Billy. 'You know as well as anybody else where my body is. It was you who made that tree fall on me.'

'It . . . it was . . . it was an accident, Billy, honest it was,' spluttered McCoyle.

'And you weren't trapped at all, Greg,' continued Billy. Greg did not reply. 'You know, they hang people for murder, but since I'm the only witness and I'm dead, I guess you won't hang. Can you both swim?' Both men dumbly shook their heads. 'Well, I guess now's as good a time as any to learn,' continued Billy, moving slowly towards them and forcing them toward the edge of the bridge. The dog also growled threateningly at them.

Both men tried pleading with Billy but he was in no mood to listen. He advanced on them very slowly, forcing them closer and closer to the edge of the bridge. At first neither of them seemed to notice this, but suddenly Ginger McCoyle looked down and grabbed at his companion. Both men looked down into the black void, knowing full well what was down there.

Billy took another step towards them, his arms outstretched, his fingers clawing the air close to their faces. Suddenly the dog snapped at Greg's ankles who then lost his footing and grabbed a tight hold of Ginger McCoyle. After a brief struggle, both men plunged off the bridge. Surprisingly, they never made a sound as they fell.

Billy thought he heard their bodies hit the water, but it was difficult to tell above the noise of the torrent. He looked down into the void for a few moments as if expecting to see something. Eventually he shrugged his shoulders, bent down and patted the dog and moved on. He was quite happy that the common verdict, when and if their bodies were discovered, would be that they were very drunk.

He thought about going back to the bunkhouse, but by that time all the other men would know what was supposed to have happened to him, and it just might save a lot of awkward questions if he were not around. Instead, he and his new friend made their way to the railroad marshalling yards where he found comparatively warm, dry, shelter between two stacks of sawn timber on one of three trains which appeared ready to move out. The dog seemed determined to stay with him and he did not object. He even gave the dog a name — Sam.

* * *

It was just breaking dawn when Billy awoke. The sudden jolt of the rail truck told him that it was being coupled up. Since he had no idea if this particular train was heading north or south, he jumped down, located the black plate on which the destination was written, compared the name to one of those he had previously copied down and was satisfied that it was destined to go through Warren Junction. The trucks jolted and started to move forward and, after a quick check that nobody was about, he leapt back on and settled down. He had never been on a train before and at first he was not at all sure if it was very safe. However, he quickly got used to it and, as it grew lighter, was even enjoying the scenery.

Billy had no real sense of time or

speed and although he had been told that Warren Junction was about forty miles away it meant very little. Later that morning as it crossed a high bridge, the train entered what was plainly a town. Billy had to assume that they had arrived in Warren Junction.

As the train crossed a wide street, Billy took the opportunity to drop off the wagon. Sam followed. He did not want anyone at the marshalling yards to see him. It was just possible they might know him.

He was quite right, they had arrived at Warren Junction and by that time Billy was feeling quite hungry. Almost opposite where he had left the train, was an establishment declaring itself to be a 'Rooming and Eating House'. If the number of customers eating was anything to go by, Billy judged that it must be popular. He went inside where nobody gave him a second glance.

'Steak an' eggs or ham an' eggs, corn hash an' coffee,' announced the large woman who appeared to be in charge.

'Ham, eggs, corn hash an' coffee for me,' said Billy. 'I guess the dog would prefer steak.'

'Fifty cents for the ham an' eggs,' said the woman holding her hand out. 'Extra coffee is five cents a mug.' She looked down at the dog and smiled. 'I got some scraps what'd suit him better. He'll have to eat out the back though.'

Billy found a one dollar note and handed it to her. 'Take for an extra coffee,' he said. 'Go with the lady, Sam,' he said to the dog. 'Wait outside for me.'

The ham was thick, well cooked and topped with three eggs. The corn hash could have been anything as far as he was concerned, but it tasted quite good and certainly better than anything he had ever had in prison. When the woman brought him his second mug of coffee, he asked her if she knew where Greenwood was and how he might get there.

'Ain't never been there,' she admitted. 'But I hear it's more'n four hundred miles north-west of here. I seem to remember there was a feller through here about a year ago askin' about Greenwood. I seem to remember him sayin' he was takin' the train west for about a hundred miles an' then headin' north. Don't know if he ever made it or not. Best person to tell you would be Jimmy Percival out at the railroad yards. He knows where every-where is.'

Having satisfied his immediate hunger and discovered who to ask, Billy decided that his first priority was to kit himself out, with help and suggestions from the store owner, with certain essentials. These included cooking pots, a sharp knife, spoon and fork, a tinder box — which the storekeeper showed him how to use — a bedroll, coffee, dried salt beef, beans, salt, flour and a large canteen which he immediately filled with water. These were his essentials. His next purchase could hardly be called essential but it was, to his mind, necessary.

Thirty years in prison had hardly gained him much experience in the use of guns and the seemingly vast array of weapons on display at the local gunsmith confused him even more. In the end he was forced to admit to the owner that he had never even held a gun during that period.

The gunsmith smiled knowingly, said that he had many customers fresh out of Sonora and suggested certain models, but it was soon very obvious that Billy was unable to handle any of them. In the end, although far more expensive than a second-hand pistol, he opted for a second-hand rifle. Including several boxes of ammunition, this purchase reduced Billy's assets by sixty dollars.

He had used a rifle in his youth but that was a long time ago. Exactly why he felt he needed a weapon of some kind, he was not really sure. It certainly was not with the intention of killing anyone and he decided it was simply self-protection.

Having made his purchases, he and Sam made their way to the marshalling yards where he eventually located Jimmy Percival.

'Greenwood,' said Percival. 'Ain't no railroad goes anywhere near there. Best way is to head out along the westbound railroad till you come to a place called Magnolia. That's about a hundred miles. Can't miss it, first stop immediately after you cross the Jackson River Canyon. From there it's about four hundred miles due north. It ain't easy goin', but it's the best way.'

Billy had no intention of using any more of his precious money purchasing a railroad ticket. He eventually worked out which was the westbound line and picked a quiet spot to wait for a freight or timber train bound in that direction. He was in luck. Within half an hour a timber train arrived. It looked identical to the one he arrived on and, selecting his wagon, he pushed Sam up first and then hauled himself up. When aboard he discovered that it was the same train and even the same wagon. He recognized one particular piece of timber by its strange graining. He had no idea what time it was, but judging by the height of the sun, it was not yet midday.

★　★　★

There was not much to do other than look at the scenery or sleep. It was still a great thrill to him to be able to see the countryside rolling by. Thirty years of the same four walls with only the occasional change of scenery being in a chain gang, made the wide world seem a wonderful place.

There were two stops during the day, both for taking on water and he managed to catch a mug of water at each stop as his wagon passed under the pipe. He drank half and gave Sam the other half. The sun was starting to set when the train crossed what he assumed must be the Jackson River Canyon and decided that he had better jump train once he was on the other side.

He had been right. Shortly after emerging from the narrow strip of woodland, he found himself on a well-used trail. There was a sign, but being unable to read, Billy had no idea what it said. However, there was an elderly man sitting outside a tumble-down cabin smoking a pipe and Billy asked him what the sign said.

'I guess it says somethin' like *Welcome to Magnolia*,' said the man, with a brood grin. 'I can't read either, son,' he continued. 'All I know for certain is that this one-horse town is Magnolia. Where you headed?'

'Greenwood,' said Billy. 'I think it's about four hundred miles north of here.'

'Probably is that at least,' agreed the old man. 'That's one hell of a way to go if you ain't got a horse.'

'I've got plenty of time,' said Billy. 'Which way do I go?'

'Best way is follow the Jackson River

for at least a day, maybe more,' said the old man. 'You'll eventually come to a place called Jackson Falls. Not much of a place. Three houses, a farm an' a tradin' post was all there was last time I was there. Don't suppose it's changed that much. Anyhow, from there the river turns east. You just keep on headin' north. I think there's a couple of small places between Jackson Falls an' Greenwood. Can't remember their names though.'

'I'll find 'em,' said Billy. 'Thanks for your help. C'mon, Sam, we got us a long walk ahead of us.'

'Poor critter's legs will be worn down to nothin',' grinned the old man. 'They ain't very long now.'

At first, following the river meant walking the edge of the gorge, but after some time the gorge disappeared and they found themselves following what seemed to be a well-worn trail alongside the river. As darkness descended Billy decided that he might as well rest up for the night.

He found a sheltered spot just above the river, lit a fire and set about preparing a meal for himself and Sam. He had had some limited experience of cooking when working in the prison kitchens. Sam, however, suddenly pricked up his ears and dashed off into the shrubbery. There was a brief yap, a growl, and Sam suddenly returned dragging a large jack rabbit, probably bigger than he was. He dropped it at Billy's feet and wagged his tail.

'Well done, Sam,' said Billy with a grin. 'Fresh meat is better'n dried salt beef any time. Now, you seem to be a very resourceful sort of guy. You don't happen to be able to cook as well do you?'

One of Billy's *essential* purchases had been a good, sharp knife. Soon the rabbit had been gutted and skinned and impaled on a stick and placed over the fire. The guts had been enjoyed by Sam, but it was apparent that he was eager for more. When it was cooked, Billy gladly shared it with his friend. Billy also made some coffee, but this was not something which Sam wanted to share. He was quite satisfied with water from the river, even though it was rather muddy looking.

The old man's prediction that it might be a day *or more* to Jackson Falls erred very much on *or more*. It was in fact the better part of three days. During that time Sam helped Billy corner and kill a small deer, which provided them with plenty of food.

# 4

The old man back in Magnolia had been right about the size of Jackson Falls. In fact when Billy and Sam showed up, their arrival appeared to double the population of both people and dogs. It was still fairly early in the afternoon and there seemed to be absolutely no reason for Billy to stay. He acknowledged an elderly woman and continued his journey. Sam showed a brief interest in a female dog, but soon decided the time was not right.

Above the falls, there was a very definite bend eastwards, also the direction of the main trail. There was a lesser trail heading north, a trail which soon petered out as Billy found himself entering flat brush land. From then on he had to concentrate on which way was north. Having no method other than the knowledge of which directions the sun rose and set, Billy found a distant mountain peak and kept it in his sights.

The wind across the plain was strong and, as night drew near, very cold. Although he sensed that there were still a couple of hours' daylight remaining, when he came across a pool of water amongst a group of large rocks and surrounded by thick thorn trees, he decided to make camp for the night. It was a good choice. They were well hidden from the biting wind and there was plenty of wood and water. He soon had a fire going. Their meal consisted of the last of the deer. Billy laid in plenty of wood for the fire and both he and Sam hardly moved all night.

The following morning Sam appeared restless and although he stayed close to Billy, he growled regularly. As far as Billy was concerned there was nothing to be seen or heard but, realizing that Sam could probably sense something he could not, he made a brief search of the area. As expected, there was nothing to be seen and he tried telling Sam to keep quiet. Sam, of course, took no notice.

For quite some time they walked in the direction of the distant peak but as they did so, Sam became even more restless and on several occasions ran off ahead, only to return even more agitated. His actions were now beginning to worry Billy and he automatically checked that his rifle was fully loaded. Not that he was capable of using it to any great effect, but it did give him some sort of comfort.

When he and Sam had cornered the deer, it was only the fact that the animal remained perfectly still for long enough for Billy to take a good aim that he was able to kill it. Had it moved, he had no doubt that he would have missed it.

How long they had been walking, Billy had no idea. Time and distance had little meaning to him. Sam had chosen that moment to once again run off and, as Billy walked past a large rock, there was a voice very close by.

'Mornin', pilgrim,' said the gruff voice. Billy turned slightly to see a man, hair covering almost all his face and dressed in what appeared to be animal hides. 'What brings a man like you walkin' this far out?' The man suddenly produced a rather ancient-looking rifle and levelled it at Billy. 'Don't try nothin', pilgrim,' he continued. He came closer and eyed Billy up and down. 'I'm a very good shot an' I can kill you before you even think about usin' that rifle. It ain't often I meets folk up here.'

'What do you want?' demanded Billy. 'I don't have nothin' of value.'

'You got a decent-lookin' rifle, nice pair of boots, just about my size I'd say,' said the man. 'Decent trousers an' jacket. I'd say that was somethin' of value. Pity you ain't got no horse or mule, that'd fetch a few dollars. Looks like you got some gear in that bag of yours as well. Now you just do as I say, strip off them clothes, an' boots an' you might just live.'

'Go to hell,' replied Billy.

'Probably will,' nodded the man. 'That's if I ain't there already — this life ain't no heaven, that's for sure. Choice is yours, pilgrim. You can either strip off or I kill you an' take 'em. Don't matter much to me either way. I just don't want to put holes in them clothes unless I have to.'

'You'd strip a man naked an' leave him to die of the cold?' asked Billy.

'A man's gotta die sometime,' said the man. 'Bullet or cold, it's all the same in the end. Least ways that's what they tell me. Now do like I say 'fore I lose my patience.'

'You were around when I started out this mornin',' said Billy. 'My dog knew there was somethin' wrong.'

'Dogs allus know when there's somethin' wrong,' said the man with a slight laugh. 'They also know when to get the hell out of it too. I seen you an' your dog. Now all I see is you. Now strip off them clothes, underwear an' all.'

'You want 'em, you take 'em,' challenged Billy.

'OK, pilgrim, if that's the way you want it,' hissed the man.

Quite suddenly, a small black and white ball shot through the air from the top of the nearby rock, landing squarely on the man's shoulders. The rifle exploded and Billy felt a sharp pain in his left shoulder. He knew he had been hit. He also remembered enough about rifles to know that the man's rifle was a single shot muzzle loader.

Ignoring the pain in his shoulder, Billy leapt forward, raised his rifle and waited for Sam to disengage himself. The moment he did so, the man raised an arm and pleaded with Billy not to shoot. Billy did not even have to think, his reaction was purely instinctive. His gun roared and a bloody hole suddenly appeared in the man's head. His eyes stared lifelessly.

'You OK, Sam?' Billy asked his dog.

'You cut that pretty fine.' Sam wagged his tail, sniffed at the now-dead body and trotted away, seeming quite pleased with himself. 'Thanks, buddy,' said Billy. 'I owe you.'

It was quite apparent, even to Billy, that the shot from the man's rifle was lodged in his shoulder. There was plenty of blood, and he could cope with that, but it did seem that the shot was pressing against the shoulder joint and was very painful when he tried to move his arm. He tore a piece of cloth from the dead man's filthy shirt and attempted to staunch the flow of blood. Eventually he packed the area with more torn cloth and covered it with his shirt and jacket.

'I need me some attention,' Billy said to Sam. 'I heard tales about things like this goin' bad ways. We need to find somewhere.'

Sam wagged his tail, barked and started to run behind the boulder. He stopped and barked again, making it obvious that Billy was to follow.

Behind the rock, in a hollow, Billy found an old, mangy-looking donkey. It had two packs on its back and Billy eventually managed to open them both slightly. They smelled quite evil and turned out to be animal hides. It seemed that the man was a hunter or trapper. There was also a smaller pack which contained powder and ball shot for the ancient rifle. There were a few cooking pots tied across the animal's battered saddle.

Billy decided that the only thing of value was the donkey itself. A search of the body produced a skinning knife, a wad of chewing tobacco and a few coins, but nothing else of interest or value. He kept the knife and the coins and threw the tobacco to one side. He also cut the skins and hides from the donkey and left them where they fell.

He looked at the body of the man and briefly wondered whether or not he ought to make some attempt to bury him, but then decided it was a waste of time and effort. He felt neither remorse nor guilt about having killed the man, and he had not felt anything when he had broken the stranger's neck or forced Ginger McCoyle and Greg from the bridge. The one thing he had seen in plenty during his time in prison was death, both natural and violent, and he had long since become hardened to it.

'Looks like we got us a ride,' Billy said to Sam as he tied his belongings to the tattered and ancient saddle. He struggled on to the animal's back, which certainly hurt his shoulder and made him sweat. When he had recovered his composure, he reached down to help Sam up. Sam simply leapt into Billy's lap, sniffed at the wound to Billy's shoulder and seemed to smile approvingly.

It had been such a long time since Billy had been astride such an animal, that at first he felt quite insecure, but he slowly got the hang of remaining on the donkey's back.

It might have been marginally more comfortable to ride than to walk, but it certainly did not seem any quicker. No matter how he tried, the donkey seemed to have only one pace — very slow. He finally abandoned trying to make it go faster and allowed it to travel at its own speed.

That evening camp was made alongside a small stream in the lea of a large rock. By that time Billy's shoulder was very painful and it became more and more difficult to even move his arm. He did manage to build a fire and to drop some salt beef and beans into a pot. He had not realized just how long such a stew took to cook and it was dark before it was finally acceptable. Sam seemed to appreciate Billy's efforts even though he himself was not so sure.

The following morning Billy felt feverish and it took most of his willpower to climb on to the donkey. Once again Sam leapt up and Billy pointed the donkey in what he thought was the right direction and was content to simply sit. Sam leapt off a couple of times during the day but otherwise kept close to Billy. He obviously sensed that all was not well.

Billy knew that it was not dark, but it was becoming increasingly difficult for him to see. Focusing was his main problem — nothing seemed to remain still long enough for him to see what it was. He was also aware that he was now sweating profusely and he felt that he had to stop and rest. Whether or not it was cold, he had no idea and even the simple act of looking for a place to stop appeared impossible . . .

$\star \quad \star \quad \star$

'You'll be OK, Mister,' said a voice close to Billy's head. 'You just take it easy.'

Billy felt warm and even secure, but he still could not bring his eyes into focus. The voice sounded like a female voice and coupled with the warmth and security of the bed he was apparently in, he felt very safe. He was quite content to obey instructions and *take it easy*.

How long it was after first hearing the voice before he was able to take any real interest in his surroundings, Billy had no idea. In fact the first indication he really had was when he felt Sam leap up and lick his face.

'Hi there, Sam,' croaked Billy. ''Nice to see you, feller. What happened?'

'You stopped a bullet in your shoulder, that's what happened,' said the female voice. 'It's been four days since we found you.'

'Four days!' croaked Billy. 'Where am I?'

'Safe for the moment,' said another voice, this time plainly older and male. 'Mary took the bullet out, she's pretty darned good at such things. She reckons if it had been left any longer gangrene would've set in. You just take it easy young feller, ain't no need to hurry.'

'*Young* feller,' said Billy. 'I'm hardly that.'

'You just listen to pa,' said the woman, Mary. 'You can ask all the questions you like when you're a bit better. After that we've got some questions of our own to ask as well.'

'It don't look like I'm goin' nowhere,' said Billy.

It was the next day before Billy felt well enough to sit up and take real note of his surroundings. He had expected to find himself in a house or cabin and was most surprised when he worked out that his bedroom was in fact a small barn and that apart from a couple of blankets, his bedding was straw. Sam was snuggled at his side. Bedroom or barn, it did not really matter to Billy, he was more than grateful for the attention he was receiving.

The woman came in carrying a bowl. She sat down in the straw beside Billy, smiled and scooped up some soup and forced him to drink. It was hot and good and Billy needed no urging to finish it off.

The woman appeared to be about his

own age, but was still a very good-looking woman. He smiled at her and took her hand in an attempt to thank her. She smiled back, blushing brightly, and slowly removed her hand from his.

'You'll be fine in a couple of days,' she said. 'You had us worried for a while. You were unconscious when we found you.'

'How did you find me?' he asked.

'I guess we didn't really,' she said with a smile. 'That dog of yours found us. Wouldn't take no for an answer. Pa almost shot him on account of he was bein' such a nuisance. Kept runnin' in an' out, barkin'. We eventually realized he was tryin' to make us go with him. We found you lyin' in half a pool of water about three miles away.'

'I'm grateful,' said Billy, 'grateful to you an' to Sam. That's the second time he's saved my life.'

'Sorry about the barn,' said Mary, looking around almost apologetically. 'We've only got a small cabin though, barely enough room for me an' pa. It's pretty warm in here though. Pa sometimes moves out here, 'specially in the summer.'

'Can I get up?' asked Billy. 'I can't lie here for the rest of my life.'

'That's up to you,' she said. 'Nobody's forcin' you to do anythin'. Take your time. Pa's out in one of the fields. I'll be in the cabin. Just one thing, pa don't like the idea of the dog bein' in the house. He reckons outside is the place for dogs.'

'That's OK,' said Billy. 'He's an outdoor sort of dog anyhow, ain't you, Sam,' he said rubbing Sam's head. 'We'll both be fine in the barn.'

'Oh, an' just one thing,' said Mary. 'You had a lot of money on you when we found you. Just don't go thinkin' we stole it. It's wrapped up in your shirt under the straw.'

'It wasn't that much,' said Billy, not really wanting to admit that he had no idea how much there was and that he could not read or count.

'Eighty-five dollars is more money

than me an' pa have seen in three years or likely to see in the next three years,' she said. 'Just lettin' you know we ain't thieves, that's all.'

'Thank you ma'am,' said Billy. 'I didn't think you were.'

'Mary's the name,' she said. 'Mary Stanton. My pa is Josh Bennett. I'm a widder woman, have been these past four years. Damn fool of a husband broke his neck fallin' off the cabin roof.'

'Sorry to hear that,' said Billy.

'Don't be,' she said with a dry laugh. 'Complete waste of time he was. Unfortunately a girl don't have much choice when it comes to men out here.'

'Children?' queried Billy.

'One stillborn, that's all,' she replied. 'I guess it just wasn't to be. Now, enough jawin' for now. I'm preparin' dinner, it'll be a couple of hours yet. You get up when you feel ready.'

She left Billy to consider his next move. It was quite apparent that he was not yet in any condition to contemplate moving on, but at the same time he did not want to outstay his welcome. Although reaching Greenwood was his objective, it did not really matter when he arrived there. After thirty years a few more weeks or even months was not going to make much difference.

Mary's father, Josh, arrived back at the cabin in midafternoon. Obviously a man well into his sixties, but at the same time very fit looking. He eyed Billy up and down for a while before suddenly taking hold of his hands and studying them rather more closely.

'They look like a fighter's hands to me,' he grunted. 'I'm a pretty good judge of these things. You must've done some fist fightin' in your time.'

'I've had me thirty years of it,' admitted Billy. He felt that there was no need to hide the fact that he had just been released from prison and the news did not appear to shock either of his hosts.

'So how did you come by that ball shot in your shoulder?' asked Josh. 'There's only one man in these parts I know who used shot like that, Silas Weekes, a filthy old trapper. I'd say that was his donkey we found you with as well. What happened, where's Silas?'

Billy explained the circumstances and the old man simply nodded. 'I guess he had it comin' to him,' he said in a matter-of-fact manner. 'It was always suspected that Silas killed a few strangers just for the clothes they stood up in. He won't be no great loss to nobody. What's your plan now?'

Once again Billy explained the reason for his being in prison and his determination to see the man responsible suffer for it. The old man nodded and said that he could understand. Mary, on the other hand, seemed to think that it had been such a long time ago that revenge seemed pointless. Billy pointed out that as far as he was concerned his time in prison meant that time, in that respect, had stood still.

'Strikes me you're goin' to need more than your fists,' said Josh. 'I see you got a rifle. Can you use it?'

'If what I'm shootin' at stands still long enough,' admitted Billy with a wry laugh. 'They don't exactly encourage the use of guns in prison, except by the guards. I guess I'll just have to learn.'

'I got me an old pistol,' said Josh. 'Come on outside, let's see how you handle it. I got me this feelin' that it's goin' to be about as much use to you as a piece of wood though.'

Billy strapped the old gunbelt to his waist and, with some instruction from Josh, practised drawing the pistol. It was very plain even to Billy that his hands were simply too big and he too inept to ever use a pistol properly.

However, over the next four days, Josh persisted and, although there was some improvement, it was certainly not enough to make Billy much of a threat to anyone except himself.

During that time Billy also felt an attraction towards Mary and it seemed that the attraction was mutual. She made no attempt to talk him out of heading for Greenwood, but there were a few times when Billy did seriously consider his position. Josh on the other hand, seemed to be looking for ways to help Billy become a better gunman.

On the morning of the fourth day of instruction, Josh suddenly produced a double-barrelled shotgun with the barrels cut down and a shortened stock. Where he had got it from even Mary had no idea. He even produced a box of twelve rather ancient-looking cartridges.

'Billy,' said Josh. 'It's plain to me that you won't rest until you've got this feller Fairfax out of your system. It's also pretty damned plain to even a blind man that you an' pistols just ain't made to go together. I reckon what I have here will solve that problem. I saw a man what had busted fingers use somethin' like this many years ago. Pretty damned effective it was too.'

'It looks a bit cumbersome,' said Billy. 'I'd probably be better off just with my rifle.'

'I was comin' to that,' said Josh. 'I've

made a special holster ... ' He produced a home-made gunbelt on which the holster had been specially enlarged to accommodate the shotgun. He had also made the holster so that there was no need to actually draw the gun. The main part of the holster swivelled.

He strapped the holster to his own waist, slipped the shotgun into it and proceeded to show Billy how to make it swivel. Billy tried it and found it quite easy to use. It sat quite well on his hips and was comfortable. Both barrels and stock were short enough to give the impression of an oversized pistol. He next tried it with a cartridge in each barrel.

The result surprised everyone. Using a sack of sand as a target, Billy suddenly swivelled the gun and blasted. The effect was devastating, the sack almost tore apart at a distance of about ten feet. Billy was very impressed and Josh also seemed very pleased with his handiwork. Mary was obviously far from impressed. She bit her lip and ran indoors.

'The one big advantage is that you don't need to be any kind of shot,' said Josh. 'Just swivel an' squeeze. Anythin' what gets in the way don't stand a chance.' He looked at Mary running to the house. 'She don't like it though,' he sighed. 'Ain't that just the way of things? She's taken quite a shine to you. You sure you want to go through with this. I could do with some help on the farm an' I ain't got nobody to leave it to 'ceptin' her an' she won't be able to manage on her own.'

Billy sighed and studied the ground for a while before replying. 'I have to,' he eventually said. 'It's been in my system for thirty years an' it ain't goin' to go away after less than thirty days. I don't know what I'm goin' to do when I finally meet up with Fairfax, I ain't never got as far as that kind of thinkin'. I reckon you know how things are. If I don't go it'll always be gnawin' away inside me.'

'Sure, I know how you feel, son,' said Josh. 'I felt the same when Mary's mother was killed. Two men turned up here while I was out. They raped Martha — Mary's mother — an' then shot her. I don't think they knew about Mary. Martha had hidden her in a drawer when they turned up. I reckon they might've killed her too, even if she was only six months old.'

'What happened to 'em?' asked Billy.

'Oh, I found 'em,' said Josh. 'It took the best part of six months but I found 'em. First I castrated 'em both then forced 'em both to eat their balls before I slit their bellies wide open.'

'Weren't you ever had up for murder?' asked Billy.

'Nope,' said Josh. 'Nobody even knew they existed an' I made sure I did it way up in the mountains where nobody hardly ever went. I did hear some years later that somebody had found two skeletons, but there was no way of tellin' who they were or how they died.'

'Did it make you feel any better?' asked Billy.

'I got one hell of a kick out of it at the time,' admitted Josh. 'Sure, it made me feel better. Just cuttin' off their balls made me feel better. I almost left it at that but I decided they might as well be dead. Don't you worry none about Mary,' he continued. 'She'll get over it if you don't want to come back. Somehow though, son, I got me this feelin' that you *will* come back. I hope I'm not wrong.'

Billy glanced at the house and nodded. 'Sure, I'll be back,' he promised.

# 5

Before leaving, Billy insisted on giving the bulk of his money to Mary and Josh, saying that it gave him another reason to come back and that he had no real use for it any longer. He actually gave them sixty dollars which Mary promised to keep until he returned — if he ever did. Josh also insisted that Billy take a large and long waterproof coat which he no longer used. He told Billy that the weather was most unpredictable at that time of year, it could rain heavily or even snow. Suitably supplied with some fresh food in the form of a piece of cooked meat, some cheese and a loaf of bread, Billy somewhat sadly took his leave. Mary advised him not to leave the meat too long.

Once again the old donkey steadfastly stuck to her own pace, but Billy did not really mind. It was another three days before he saw any indication that he was not alone in the world.

The sign obviously pointed to a settlement of some kind, the arrow was plain enough even if he could not read the name. Eventually he arrived in a small town which straddled a shallow river. He learned that it was called Clearwater.

His arrival seemed to cause a great deal of amusement, particularly amongst the children and was plainly more to do with the mode of transport and the fact that he had a dog riding with him than anything else. He simply smiled and ignored the comments.

He tethered the donkey to a drinking trough, Sam jumped down and immediately disappeared and Billy decided that a drink of beer would not come amiss. However, he did notice that two men appeared to be taking rather more than a healthy interest in him. Immediately he thought about the two strangers sent to Sonora to make certain he never reached Greenwood.

His hand slipped to his hip and the stock of his new gun. He felt strangely secure. He made a mental note of what the two men looked like and entered the only saloon in town.

'Greenwood,' he said to the bartender. 'How far?'

'On that thing you're ridin',' came the reply with a laugh, 'I'd say about another four weeks.'

'Greenwood's about three hundred miles, maybe more,' said a man leaning against the counter. 'Ted's right about how long it's goin' to take though. It's slow enough on a horse, but that thing of yours is sure to take about four weeks. Donkeys only go at one pace — dead slow, but I guess you know what. Now if it's a decent horse you're lookin' for, I'm just your man. I got me three good horses, best horseflesh you'll find anywhere.'

'Ain't nothin' wrong with my donkey,' said Billy, handing over some money and allowing and trusting the bartender to take the correct amount.

'OK, so it takes four weeks, I ain't in no hurry.'

'Can't afford a horse, you mean,' sneered the man. 'What you want to go to Greenwood for? Ain't nothin' in Greenwood. I was there about six months ago. Ain't nothin' but cattle an' a few farms.'

'Not much different from this place then,' responded Billy. 'Nothin' but rocks, trees an' one saloon.'

'And gold,' said the man. 'You don't look like a miner though. You're big enough but you don't look the type.'

'Too much like hard work,' said Billy, not really knowing much about gold or looking for it.

'So what's in Greenwood?' the man asked again.

'I got me some unfinished business,' said Billy. 'Is Mr Fairfax still more-or-less runnin' the town?'

'Fairfax!' said the man, somewhat surprised. 'Sure, he's still there. You're right about him runnin' the place, I heard he owns most of the town an' county. You know Fairfax then?'

'I know Fairfax,' grunted Billy. 'We go back a long time.' He drained his glass. 'Thanks for the information. By the way, there was two men outside lookin' at me in a strange sort of way, an' I don't mean 'cos of my donkey. Any ideas who they might be? I get nervous when men look at me like that.'

The bartender glanced at the door and then at Billy. 'I know who you mean,' he said. 'Strangers in town, been here for three days now. I'd say they was waitin' for somebody. Maybe they're waitin' for you, but I wouldn't've thought so. I'd also say they was takin' an interest in you on account of that piece of artillery hangin' at your side,' he said. 'I ain't never seen nothin' like that before.'

Billy rested his hand on the stock and gave a broad grin. 'I ain't sure what artillery means but this piece will blast anyone full of holes within ten yards.'

Billy ignored further questioning as to why he had to wear such a piece and went out on to the street. The two men were still there, only this time they tried to look as though they were not interested in him. However, Billy detected a brief nudge between the men and they wandered off. He waited for a while, watching them disappear into a rooming house. He had the distinct feeling that he had not seen the last of them.

Since it was still early afternoon and he had no particular reason to remain in Clearwater, Billy decided to carry on. He mounted his donkey, looked around for Sam but could not see him and decided that the dog would probably catch him up. He was right — he had hardly passed the last building before Sam raced up and jumped up into his lap.

He rode on until the first signs of nightfall when he found a suitable place to rest for the night. He looked back, half expecting to see the two men from Clearwater following him, but there was no sign of them. He wondered if he was allowing his imagination to get the better of him and that the men were not at all interested in his movements.

It was completely dark when Sam, who had been lying alongside him, suddenly picked up his head and growled. This time Billy knew better than to ignore him.

'Go find 'em, Sam,' Billy whispered.

Sam needed no second bidding and ran off behind some rocks. In the meantime Billy remembered something an old convict had told him. He unfolded the waterproof coat, removed his hat, found three branches and draped the coat over two of them and his hat on the other, making it look as though he was sitting by the fire. He then hid himself behind a large rock and waited.

About five minutes passed before Billy became aware of movement a few yards away to his right and two shadowy figures eased themselves from behind a rock. Suddenly there were several shots, the hat flew off its stick and the two figures rushed forward.

One of the men swore as he kicked the coat and both immediately crouched low, guns drawn. Billy remained where he was as he spoke.

'Sorry to disappoint you,' he rasped. 'I can see you against the fire, but I don't think you can see me. Hold it right where you are. This gun of mine might not be a pistol but I can assure you from this distance it can blow your heads off, both at the same time. Drop your guns and stand up. Nice and easy now.' Both men obeyed, dropped their guns and slowly stood up, arms raised. 'That's better,' said Billy. 'Now I got a couple of questions to ask.'

'Nice trick,' said one of them. 'I guess that dog of yours picked upon us bein' here. We should've allowed for that.'

'But you didn't,' said Billy. 'Now, who sent you?'

'I reckon you already know the answer,' said one of them. 'You *are* Billy Nesbitt, ain't you?'

'Might be,' said Billy. 'Who wants to know?'

'Mr James Fairfax from Greenwood,' said the other. 'Don't ask us why, but he wants you dead.'

'Oh, I know why,' said Billy. 'Seems he must really want me dead, this is the second time somebody's tried an' the second time they've failed. How'd you know I was comin' this way?'

'He said there was no other way you could come,' said one. 'He had a wire from some place called Sonora, that's all we know.'

'The two men he sent there to kill me obviously didn't succeed as you can see,' said Billy, stepping from behind the rock and moving a couple of yards closer, his gun now in his hands. 'One of 'em is dead, I broke his neck. I don't know what happened to the other one an' I don't really care that much. Now it don't matter to me if I kill you or not, choice is yours. How much is Fairfax payin' you?'

'Two hundred,' said one. 'If we take

your body back.'

'Two hundred,' said Billy. 'He must be really desperate. I hear there's a good many outlaws ain't worth that much. It looks like you wasted your time though. I suppose I ought to kill you. I would if I had any sense, it'd mean two less to bother about. If I don't kill you I'll be always lookin' behind me, not knowin' where you were.'

Suddenly Sam was rushing at the ankles of one of the men and Billy caught a glint of metal in the man's hand. He had obviously drawn another gun. The gun fired but the bullet was well wide. Sam disappeared and one of the two barrels of Billy's gun roared. The man cried out in agony, clutched at his chest and fell to the ground where he writhed about for some time.

'Told you this thing was lethal,' said Billy to the other man. 'You got any ideas of doin' the same? There's two barrels an' I only used one, remember. Care to take a chance?'

'Don't shoot,' pleaded the man. 'I seen what a mess a gun like that can make of a man, even if it don't kill him. I seen a man's face blasted half away an' he still lived. I'd rather be dead than look like that.'

The man on the ground moaned and moved slightly.

'Looks like he ain't dead,' said Billy. 'Like you say though, he sure will be a mess. I can see the bone in his jaw. OK, I ain't about to shoot you if you don't try nothin' an' do what I tell you. I might be makin' a mistake but that's a chance I'll have to take. Get your friend out of here, take him back to Fairfax an' tell that son-of-a-bitch that he'll have to do better than he has so far. Billy Nesbitt don't die so easy after thirty years. You can also tell him that I'll be back in Greenwood sometime. I can't say when, I ain't in no hurry, not after thirty years of waitin'. He'll know what I mean an' him not knowin' just when I'll show up will make him sweat. I wish I could be there to see that. You can tell him to watch his back. I could be waitin' behind a rock or a tree when he least expects it. No matter how many men like you he sends out, I'll be there sometime when I'm good an' ready.'

'Sure thing,' gulped the man. He indicated the man on the ground. 'Exceptin' I ain't takin' him with me. This was all his idea anyhow an' I don't intend dyin' for him or Fairfax, two hundred dollars or not.'

The man on the ground suddenly gave a loud cry, arched his back and fell back, emitting a deep groan. Then there was silence.

'I'd say he was dead,' said Billy, dispassionately. 'OK, unless you want some of the same, get the hell out of here before I change my mind. Just remember to tell Fairfax.'

'Yes, sir,' said the man, trying to find his gun on the ground.

'No gun,' ordered Billy. 'You leave 'em where they are, just get goin'. I'm goin' to count to ten, if you ain't disappeared by then you get this other barrel.'

There was no need for Billy to even start counting. The man raced into the darkness, followed by Sam who yapped and snapped at his heels. Eventually Sam returned looking very pleased with himself and Billy heard the sound of a horse being ridden away.

'Looks like we might've gained ourselves a horse,' said Billy. 'Let's go see.'

However, although he found where the horse had been left, there was no sign of a second horse. Billy shrugged and smiled to himself. He ought to have realized that the man could take both animals.

After checking that the man was indeed dead, Billy pulled the body to one side and some distance away and searched it for anything of value or use. Apart from the gunbelt and the three guns, there was nothing of value. He kept the guns and the gunbelt on the basis that he might be able to sell them.

He even considered removing the man's clothes, but decided that they were now too full of holes and too bloodstained. He stoked up the fire and settled down. There were no further disturbances that night.

Whether or not the other man *would* return to Greenwood did not really bother Billy. He reasoned that if neither man showed up, Fairfax would know that something had gone wrong. Either way, he knew Fairfax would get the message loud and clear.

For another three days they slowly made their way across open plains. On the second day it rained heavily and both Billy and Sam were more than grateful for the large waterproof coat which also covered most of the donkey. Whether or not the donkey appreciated that fact was impossible to tell. For the most part Sam kept himself snuggled on Billy's lap, only occasionally pushing his nose or head through between buttons. On the third day they came across a farmhouse where Billy offered to buy some bread and some fresh meat for Sam.

The farmer and his wife were both rather surly and obviously most uncertain about Billy. The man never put his shotgun down and was plainly ready to use it. They did, however, agree to sell Billy two loaves of bread — which were stale — and a large leg of cooked mutton. Billy had no idea how much they charged him and they seemed to know that he could not count. Whatever the amount, it appeared to take most of his remaining money. He chose not to argue the point.

It seemed that the man he had allowed to go free had also passed that way but at least a day and a half ahead of Billy. Yes, he had had two horses. They also told him that the next town was at least two days away at the speed he travelled and was called Clinton. Not a big town by all accounts, but it had everything a man might need including a whorehouse and a timber mill. Billy fingered what was left of his money and wondered if he might get a few days' work at the mill. He would think about it as he travelled.

Clinton was a town slightly larger than most, about the same size as Sonora. It had three saloons and, as he had been told, a whorehouse. He was certainly not interested in the whorehouse despite the urgings and far-from-subtle invitations by scantily clad women. By then his priority was the need for more supplies and he went into a general store where he admitted to the owner that he could not read, write or count, showed him what money he had and asked him how much he had.

'Eight dollars an' thirty-two cents,' said the store owner. 'That ain't goin' to get you very far.'

'Maybe I can get a couple of day's work at the mill,' said Billy. 'I'm used to handlin' timber.'

'You can try,' said the store owner. 'Don't think you'll have much luck though. There's other men lookin' for work an' they can't get none. What provisions do you need?'

'The usual I guess,' said Billy. 'Flour, coffee, salt, sugar maybe, dried meat an' beans. I got me three guns an' a gunbelt, can you take them in payment?'

'Don't deal in guns,' said the owner. 'There's a gunsmith's down the street, next to the barber's shop. You can try there. I can do you a pound of flour, pound of coffee, half a pound of salt, a pound of sugar, two pounds of beans an' five pounds of salt beef for six dollars. That leaves you two dollars an' thirty-two cents. Like I said, that won't get you far.'

'I'll manage,' said Billy. 'Put them up for me, I'll go see if I can sell those guns. I'll be back.'

Billy found the gunsmith who carefully examined the three pistols and the belt. Eventually he slowly shook his head.

'Old pieces,' he said. 'Ain't much demand for old pieces like these. As a matter of fact I've got me a drawer full of pieces like this. Folk come into town lookin' for work an' usually end up sellin' their guns. Mostly they are old pieces like these. These days I seem to be buyin' more guns than I sell. Sorry, I can't give you much for these. Ten dollars the lot an' no hagglin'.' He opened a drawer and showed Billy that it was almost full of guns. 'See what I mean,' he continued. 'Ten dollars, take it or leave it, I don't care which.'

'OK,' sighed Billy. 'Ten dollars it is.'

He took the money and returned to collect his supplies from the general store. He loaded them on to his donkey and looked about for Sam, who had long since disappeared. He was outside a saloon and, having acquired something of a taste for beer, decided to spend a few cents of his precious money.

There were three men lounging at the bar who looked Billy up and down, sneered at him and then laughed amongst themselves. They were big men, one of them rather larger than Billy.

'Lost your dog?' sneered one of them. 'Last I seen of him he was sniffin' round a bitch. Only trouble was the bitch was too far off the ground for him.'

'I guess he'll manage,' said Billy, as he ordered his beer.

'I'd say that donkey of yours is just about the right height for you though,' said the largest man with a coarse laugh. 'I heard stories about men who ride donkeys. I hear they prefer humpin' their donkeys to a woman.'

'I guess you ought to know,' said Billy, bracing himself for the trouble he sensed was about to come. 'They do say them what talk about it must know what it's like to do it.'

'Are you sayin' I'm a donkey . . . ?'

'That's what I *am* sayin',' said Billy, interrupting before the man had finished speaking.

'Mister,' snarled the man, straightening up and turning to face Billy. He was at least three inches taller with broader shoulders and a larger chest. He was not a man to be tangled with under normal circumstances. 'That's what I call fightin' talk,' he continued. 'Now I want an apology from you an' a beer for me an' my friends just to show you didn't mean it.'

'No apology an' no beer,' said Billy, steeling himself for trouble. It was nothing more than pure awkwardness which made him act that way.

'I don't think I made myself plain,' said the man, stepping up to Billy. 'I said I want an apology an' a beer each for me an' my friends.'

'I heard you the first time,' said Billy. 'I don't think you heard me properly. I said no apology an' no beer.'

Suddenly the man's fist lashed out, but Billy had been expecting something like that. He easily rode the punch and at the same time his fist crashed into the man's face. The man dropped to the floor, blood streaming from his nose. He appeared to be unconscious. The other two squared up to Billy but did not seem anxious to strike out first.

'I guess you just got lucky,' snarled one of them. 'You're the only man I've met who ever put Silas down. Like I say, you just got lucky. I'll bet you couldn't beat him in a proper fist fight. Nobody has ever beaten him.'

'Maybe I could, maybe I couldn't,' said Billy. 'One of you care to take his place. I'll take both of you at the same time if you like.'

The bartender intervened, ordering the two men to get Silas out of the saloon. When they had dragged him outside, he turned to Billy.

'They was right about you bein' the only man ever to put Silas down,' he said. 'I had the feelin' that you were handy with your fists. Care to try an' earn yourself fifty dollars?'

'What man wouldn't be interested in that kind of money,' said Billy. 'Who do I have to kill?'

'Nobody,' replied the bartender. 'All you have to do is fight Silas in a fair fight. Winner gets fifty dollars.'

'When?' asked Billy.

'Tomorrow afternoon,' said the bartender. 'It's Sunday, the day when we usually have fist fights. It ain't often somebody wants to try an' take on Silas. You are just about the best prospect I've seen in a long time. I might even risk a few dollars on you myself.'

Billy considered the offer for a few moments. 'OK, I guess I ain't got nothin' to lose an' I could do with the money. I'll leave it to you to fix things. By the way, did a man with two horses pass this way?'

'Sure did, seemed to be in a hurry as well,' said the bartender. 'He sold one of the horses an' the saddle down at the livery. Him an' another feller passed through a few days earlier headin' south. He never said what happened to the other man. Friend of yours?'

'Nope, just curious about the man,' said Billy. 'Which way did he go?'

'East,' said the bartender.

East — that meant that he was not going back to Greenwood.

That night Billy and Sam spent the night camped just outside town. There was no trouble and when Billy returned to the saloon later in the morning, he learned that a fight between him and Silas McGuire had been arranged for two o'clock that afternoon in a paddock behind the livery stable.

Billy had no idea what the time was, but when crowds started to gather outside the livery, he guessed that it must be about time. Already some wagers were changing hands, although most folk seemed not prepared to bet against Silas McGuire. Those who were putting their money on Billy had obviously been influenced by the bartender. Who was putting up the money for the fight, Billy never discovered and did not care.

Eventually Silas McGuire arrived and stripped off to the waist which made him look even bigger. Billy started to have some doubts about the wisdom of agreeing to the fight, but decided that it was too late to back out.

The two men were called together where the rules, such as they were, were explained to them. Silas glared hatred at Billy and as soon as the referee pushed them apart prior to the start of the fight, he growled all kinds of obscenities at Billy, vowing that revenge would be swift and very, very painful.

The fight commenced with Silas rushing at Billy, plainly intent on an early victory. However, Billy side-stepped, stuck out his leg and watched with some satisfaction as Silas crashed headlong into the dirt, much to the delight of the crowd, even those who had not wagered any money on Billy.

Silas looked up in obvious surprise, shook his head and struggled to his feet. This time he did not rush in, but slowly plodded towards Billy. Billy had already decided that McGuire's weak spot was his nose, from their previous encounter. McGuire closed in and a blow glanced off Billy's head but did not cause any problem. His fist slammed hard into McGuire's stomach. Any normal man would have buckled under such a blow, but it hardly seemed to register on McGuire. That decided Billy, he would concentrate on the man's face. For about five minutes, they traded blows, Billy prepared to take some punches in order to create an opening. However, apart from one blow to McGuire's face which plainly caused him a great deal of pain, the big man did not give Billy too many opportunities. In the meantime Billy took a great number of blows in the stomach and chest and whilst they did not put him down, they were nevertheless very painful.

A sudden unexpected blow to Billy's head sent him crashing to the ground and hurt more than any other blow. With the roar of the crowd ringing in his ears, Billy managed to struggle to his feet again, only to be immediately sent flying backwards once again to the dirt by another blow to his head. It was plain that the crowd sensed the fight was almost over. Billy, however, remembering the fifty dollars, had other ideas.

Once again on his feet, Billy rode several punches when quite unexpectedly McGuire's unprotected leering face loomed large in front of him. With all the force he could muster, Billy's fist slammed into that face.

McGuire went down, briefly struggled to his feet, encouraged by the crowd, only to be met once again by Billy's fist. This time McGuire could not get off the ground and was counted out. There were boos from the majority of the crowd and a few cheers from those who had wagered on Billy. Billy sat down to recover with Sam licking his wounds. He was now fifty dollars the richer.

# 6

Billy was in the saloon later that evening when McGuire and his two companions came in. Immediately Billy feared the worst and made himself ready for trouble. It appeared that most of the other occupants also expected trouble with those closest to Billy quickly moving to one side. They did not leave, they did not want to miss another fight between the pair.

'That should've been *my* fifty dollars,' muttered McGuire as he placed his huge bulk alongside Billy. His companions took position on the other side. 'You intend stoppin' long?' he asked.

'I'll be on my way in the mornin',' said Billy. 'There ain't no reason for me to stay here any longer'n I have to.'

Suddenly McGuire grinned, showing a mouthful of blackened teeth. 'Ain't no need to if'n you don't want to,' he said. 'I don't hold no grudge, you won that fight fair an' square.' He turned to the others in the room. 'You all hear that,' he called. 'Billy here won that fight fair an' square an' don't let me hear nobody say he didn't.' There was a surprised murmur round the room. 'This time though,' he said turning once again to Billy, 'I reckon you *do* owe me a beer. You can afford it now.'

'Sure thing,' agreed Billy, surprised and pleased at the way things had turned out. He ordered three glasses of beer. 'I thought you might've been mad at me.'

'Naw!' said McGuire, slapping Billy hard on the back, which made Billy splutter. 'You're the best fighter I've ever seen apart from a feller called Curly Kabbanitch. Most folk called him Cabbage, but he didn't like that. He beat me once an' I beat him once.'

'And I beat him once,' said Billy. 'I was up against him in Sonora.'

'Yeh, I can believe you did beat

Curly,' said McGuire with a laugh. 'So, he's in Sonora now. Maybe I'll go there an' make it the best of three.' He looked about the room and lowered his head close to Billy's. 'Just a word of warnin',' he said quietly. 'There was a feller through here vowin' to kill you. He reckoned you'd killed his friend an' that he'd been offered two hundred dollars to make sure you never reached Greenwood.'

'I thought he went off east,' said Billy.

'That's what folk were supposed to think,' said McGuire. 'I know he turned up north. I reckon he might be waitin' for you somewhere between here an' Greenwood. I like you, you're a good fighter. I'd hate to see a good fighter like you get on the wrong end of a bullet.'

'Thanks for the warnin',' said Billy. 'I can't say as I'm too surprised.'

'Two hundred dollars,' mused McGuire. 'If you had been any other man I might've had a go at collectin' that myself.'

★　★　★

Billy was on his way almost as soon as dawn broke. When he had settled down for the night there had been no sign of Sam, but when he awoke he found the dog asleep at his side. He had purchased a few more supplies the previous day, including a large piece of cooked meat which had seen better days, but which Sam seemed to appreciate. There was nobody to witness his departure and in a way he was thankful for that.

Now that he knew there was somebody ahead of him and wanting to kill him, Billy proceeded with rather more caution than usual. The first day was through thickly forested, steep-sided, narrow valleys and his route was determined purely by the terrain. Ambush was quite possible at almost any point and he talked to Sam about it. He did not really think that the dog understood a single word, but it made him feel better.

Whether or not Sam *did* understand was open to question. After having his talking to, Sam frequently leapt off the donkey and disappeared. He would return a few minutes later and leap back on Billy's lap. All the time he was doing just that, Billy felt reasonably safe.

There were three occasions during the day when Sam reacted to something but on each occasion it turned out to be perfectly natural. The first was a large, lone wolf, which soon disappeared, the second a deer and the third a huge bear. The bear gave Billy most cause for concern. He knew from his distant youth that his shotgun was no earthly use against such an animal. He still had the rifle but even that, barring a very lucky shot, would not stop a rampaging bear.

For a time the bear blocked the road ahead, standing on all fours and swaying slightly from side to side as it eyed the donkey and Billy. Sam had disappeared into the forest at first sight of the bear, probably because he knew that was the safest place to be. For her part, the donkey appeared as though she had not even seen the bear. For a few minutes bear and Billy eyed each other warily. Suddenly the bear let out a low growl and lumbered off into the forest. Billy breathed a sigh of relief. A short time later Sam returned and Billy teased him for being a coward.

Their journey through the forest lasted three days. After the first day, the valleys widened and on the third day they seemed to disappear completely. During that time Billy succeeded in killing two large birds with a single shot from his shotgun and Sam found the carcass of a recently dead deer. It appeared to have fallen from a high ledge and broken its neck. It must have been very recent as the carcass was still warm and the scavengers had not yet found it. The meat appeared edible and Billy sliced off several portions for both himself and Sam. The deer meat tasted fine, but the birds were very tough and tasted rather peculiar. He decided that he would not kill any more birds.

In all that time, although he had kept a constant vigil, there was no sign of the man sent to kill him. He was rather surprised, the forest had seemed to him to be an ideal place for ambush. Halfway through the afternoon of the fourth day, the forest petered out completely and Billy found himself on a rolling plain dotted with clumps of trees.

Since leaving Clinton, Billy had seen no signs of human life but now, in the distance, he thought he could make out a house or farm or group of houses. Whatever it was, Billy decided to head for it, even though it was slightly away from the direction he had set himself.

It turned out to be what seemed a long-abandoned settlement. Most of the buildings were in an advanced state of decay and grass and weeds had taken over almost every bit of open ground. He did find a water pump which, very surprisingly, worked at the first stroke of the handle.

He pushed his head under the flowing water and then suddenly stood up straight. It had just registered on him why the pump had worked first time. The ground below the nozzle had been wet and obviously recently so. He looked about, knowing that he was not alone.

'Where is he, Sam?' he whispered to the dog. 'Go find him.'

Despite Billy's doubts, Sam *did* appear to understand and raced off to search the various buildings. He did manage to disturb several rats, one of which he killed, and a flock of pigeons, but nothing else.

Billy was quite satisfied that the man was not in the immediate vicinity but was also quite certain that he was not too far away. He scanned the land ahead, hoping to catch a telltale sign. There was nothing to be seen. Since it was by that time late afternoon, he decided that he might as well rest up for the night. He had good shelter and plenty of water.

He found himself a cabin which was not quite as dilapidated as the others and which had a stone fireplace. The night passed uneventfully.

The following morning, Billy quite deliberately did not start out until the sun was reasonably high. From then on he kept a constant lookout for any signs and even Sam appeared to be more alert than usual.

They travelled for at least an hour during which time Sam was hardly with him, continually racing off ahead. Normally the dog returned and seemed to indicate that all was well, but on the final occasion he returned and was obviously rather more agitated.

Ahead of them were a group of boulders and there was little alternative but to continue through them. The closer they got to them, the more agitated Sam became. Billy stopped about a hundred yards short of the rocks and carefully examined them.

There was still nothing to indicate that anyone was there, but Sam's behaviour convinced Billy that his would-be assassin was definitely amongst them.

He was hidden by a clump of trees and, after some consideration, decided that the best thing he could do would be to leave the donkey amongst the trees and make his way forward on foot and hope to surprise the man. Sam obviously had his own ideas and raced off.

Approaching the rocks without being seen appeared impossible from all angles except one. This, however, involved a detour which would bring him to the rocks almost from the opposite direction. He tethered the donkey, took his rifle with him and set off, taking care to keep well out of sight. It was not that he had much faith in his ability to use the rifle, but that was something which the man waiting would not know.

Eventually, quite certain that he had not been seen, Billy found himself looking down on the rocks. At first he could not see anyone, but then a slight movement fixed the position of the man. As far as Billy could see, it *was* the man he had allowed to go free. He now regretted that decision.

Billy moved round slightly and was able to get a better view of the man. He appeared to be concentrating on the direction from which he expected Billy to come. Billy moved down the slope and as slowly and as quietly as possible made his way forward.

All would probably have been well had it not been for Sam. Billy was within about thirty yards of the man and still unnoticed when the dog suddenly raced from behind a rock. The man saw the dog, attempted to shoot it but failed and then seemed to realize that Billy was behind him. A shot ricocheted off a nearby rock, forcing Billy to duck and when he looked again the man had disappeared.

'Nice try,' a voice echoed round, making it almost impossible to fix his position. 'That damned dog of yours again. Don't worry, I won't let you get close enough to use that cannon of yours. Looks like I got the edge this time, even if you did try sneakin' up on me. I know exactly where you are but you don't know where I am. I can afford to wait an' pick you off. Look behind you, Nesbitt, I might be there or I just might be right in front of you. Oh, an' don't rely on that damned dog of yours again. First chance I get I'm goin' to kill him.'

Sam had disappeared again and Billy had no idea where he was. He silently willed Sam to keep well out of the way.

'I should've killed you while I had the chance,' called Billy. 'It ain't a mistake I'll make again.'

'Maybe you should've,' agreed the man. 'I'm grateful to you for that but you're worth two hundred dollars to me so don't expect me to be too grateful. You won't get a second chance. Just one thing. How the hell did you know I was here? I know it wasn't that dog of yours this time.'

'Water,' replied Billy.

'Water!' came the reply. 'What the hell are you talkin' about?'

'That abandoned settlement,' said Billy. 'The ground under the water pump was wet, freshly wet too an' the pump worked first time. That told me somebody had used it recently an' the only man I could think of was you. You ought to be more careful.'

'We all make mistakes,' said the man with a coarse laugh. 'Still, it don't matter now. Pity you had to kill my partner, we'd been together a long time. In a way though maybe it was a good thing. This way I get to keep the whole two hundred.'

'You ain't killed me yet,' said Billy.

'Not yet,' agreed the man. 'But my rifle against your shotgun? No contest I'd say. All I've got to do is keep out of range of that shotgun of yours, which shouldn't be too hard. Close-to that gun of yours might be lethal but any

141

more'n about twenty feet an' it's next to useless.'

Unfortunately for Billy, he knew that the man was quite right. He did have a rifle, which the man obviously did not know about, but Billy also knew that his chances of using it effectively were almost zero. He had to get closer to be able to use his shotgun. The problem was that he did not know exactly where the man was, although he had by that time established a general direction.

He looked about and tried to move but was immediately forced to duck again as another bullet ricocheted off a nearby rock. He appeared to be pinned down. He picked up a piece of rock and tossed it to his right. There was no reaction other than a coarse laugh.

'You'll have to do better'n that, my friend,' the man laughed. 'I'm used to all them kind of tricks.'

Billy decided that it was time to let the man know that he too had a rifle. The fact that he hardly knew how to use it effectively and the only bullets he had brought with him were those already loaded did not matter, the man would not know. He very slowly eased himself up between two rocks, pointed the rifle in the general direction he thought his assailant was and fired. For some reason he automatically closed his eyes as he did so. The effect was much better than he could ever have hoped.

'Jeez!' came the cry. 'I didn't know you had a rifle.'

'I can use it too,' bluffed Billy. 'Might not be much use with a pistol, but I sure can use a rifle.'

There was no reply but suddenly Sam was racing past Billy, yapping loudly. A few moments later Billy heard the sound of a horse being ridden away. There was a single shot, which Billy guessed was aimed at Sam. Eventually however, Sam returned looking very pleased with himself.

Billy stood and watched as the man disappeared into the distance and then, more or less at the insistence of Sam, looked where the man had hidden.

There was a dark patch of what was obviously blood. It appeared that his shot had somehow injured the man.

Now quite certain that nobody was lying in ambush for him, Billy continued his journey.

About halfway through that afternoon, Sam suddenly growled and at the same time Billy saw a horse standing alone on the trail about a hundred yards away. Cautious as ever, Billy dismounted, Sam raced off and Billy slowly made his way forward on foot. What he saw surprised even him.

A man was lying on the ground a short distance behind the horse. He was not moving but Billy did not go too close. His shotgun was now held, swivelled in its holster, ready to use. Sam reached the body before Billy did and sniffed at it without any reaction from the man. Billy moved forward.

There was no question of it, it *was* the same man he had allowed to go free but there was also no question that he was now dead. His clothing and chest were stained a deep red and already flies in abundance were around the blood. It was quite obvious that Billy's shot had been extremely lucky and had hit the man in the chest. It seemed that the exertion of riding had made him bleed even more and he had lost a lot of blood.

'Guess there's nothin' I can do for you now,' muttered Billy. 'I'll take your rifle an' whatever else you might have. It looks like I found me a horse as well.'

He removed the man's empty gun-belt — it was always possible he might be able to sell it — checked the man's pockets where he found money in the form of two notes and some coin. He had no idea how much it was and did not care. In the saddle-bag he found some rope, a knife and spoon and a box of bullets for the rifle. There were also a cooking pot and billycan and a few provisions in the form of flour, coffee and beans tied to the saddle.

It also appeared that at last Billy had gained a faster form of transport than his donkey, although by that time he had grown quite attached to the animal. He tried to mount the horse, however, it seemed that the horse did not want to co-operate. It bucked and shied, leaving Billy in a heap on the ground.

It was only after the third attempt that Billy remembered that the last time he had ridden a horse was when he had been a youth of sixteen — thirty years previously. Even then, the only horse he had ever ridden had been a large, broad-backed working horse belonging to his father. He laughed to himself as he realized that he must be the only man in the whole of America who was unable to ride a horse.

He had seen men riding horses and had never given the matter much thought, considering it a natural thing. However, he was quite determined that he was not going to be beaten by any horse. He tried mounting again.

On this occasion he succeeded and at first managed to remain in the saddle, despite the obvious protests of the horse. It seemed however, that the horse was very single minded about some things and was not going to submit too easily.

Quite suddenly the animal was racing forward and Billy could not control it. In a matter of seconds he found himself once again on the ground nursing a sore arm, and looked up to see the horse tossing its head and snorting. It seemed as if it found the spectacle quite funny.

'OK, OK, you win,' grumbled Billy. 'I ain't leavin' you out here though. I should be able to sell you an' that saddle.'

The horse allowed Billy to take the reins and lead it back to the donkey where it was tied to the donkey's saddle. Billy mounted the donkey and discovered that he felt much safer and was far happier riding the smaller animal. Sam, as ever, jumped up into his lap and the strange group slowly made its way forward.

★ ★ ★

For four more days they crossed plain and woodland. During that time there was no sign of human life. Water was no problem and meat, in the form of rabbit put up by Sam and eventually shot by Billy and then a very young deer, once again found by Sam. Billy felt quite sorry for the young deer; it made no attempt to move as Billy used his rifle, taking very careful aim, to kill it.

The rabbit had obviously not been a young animal and the tough meat was not helped by the fact that it was now full of shot. Billy removed as much of the shot as he could but still discovered plenty as he ate the meat. Sam appeared largely untroubled by the shot.

Halfway through the morning of the fifth day, as they were descending a steep bank, Billy saw a town straddling a river below them, about a couple of miles away. At first he wondered if he had reached Greenwood. That too straddled a river but he could not remember the hills he was now descending. The fact he could not read did not help when he eventually came across a sign obviously declaring the name of the town.

Having had men waiting for him before, Billy entered the town looking for someone who was plainly looking for him. This time he did not see anybody.

The fact that he arrived riding a donkey and leading a horse caused a certain amount of laughter but he simply ignored it. His first call was to what appeared to be the only livery stable.

'Now I done seen everythin',' said the blacksmith with a coarse laugh. 'A man comes into town, ridin' a moth-eaten old donkey, leadin' a perfectly good horse an' wants to sell the *horse*! You gone loco or summat?'

'Somethin' like that,' agreed Billy. 'Let's just say I prefer ridin' my donkey. I ain't no real judge of horse-flesh but

I'd say this was a good animal. You want to buy her or not?'

The blacksmith cast his experienced eye over the animal, examined its teeth and eyes and seemed satisfied. Billy was quite surprised that the horse had allowed the blacksmith to handle it as he had done. He knew full well had it been him who had tried those things the horse would have tried to bite him. Indeed, it had tried to bite and kick him on several occasions during their journey.

'Forty dollars,' said the blacksmith. 'Ten dollars for the saddle, fifty dollars in all. How does that sound? Don't matter much to me if you don't like it, take it or leave it.'

Whether or not he was supposed to haggle, Billy did not know. He felt that he might have been able to stick out for more, but fifty dollars seemed a fair price so he accepted it. The rifle he had taken off the dead man, although the same make and calibre as his own, was the better of the two, so he kept that one and decided to sell the other. He took the rifle along to a nearby gunsmith where he sold both rifle and gunbelt for another thirty dollars. In return he bought a box of twelve cartridges for his shotgun.

'I'm headed for Greenwood,' Billy said to the gunsmith. 'How far?'

'Hundred an' fifty, maybe a hundred an' seventy miles,' said the gunsmith. 'Just keep on headin' north. You'll have to cross a range of mountains about halfway but it should be easy enough. If the snow's arrived early it might be harder, but even so it ain't too bad.' He looked at the sawn-off shotgun at Billy's side and smiled. 'I seen a man wearin' a gun just like that many years ago,' he said. 'Mighty effective close-to as well. He had two busted hands an' couldn't use a regular gun properly so he came up with that idea. Your hands don't look busted, what's your excuse?'

'Too big, too clumsy,' said Billy with a grin. He raised both hands, clenched his fists and then punched the air.

'More used to beatin' the hell out of a man than usin' guns,' he continued. 'I'm what they call a bare-knuckle fighter.'

'Sure, I can see that now,' agreed the gunsmith. 'If it's a fight you're lookin' for I reckon you're in the wrong part of the country. I hear fist fightin' is quite a big thing further south among the miners an' lumber men.'

'I know,' said Billy. 'I've just come from there.'

'One thing's for certain,' said the gunsmith, 'you won't find no fist fighters up in Greenwood.'

'I ain't lookin' for fist fighters,' said Billy, 'just a man called James Fairfax. You heard of him?'

'I reckon everybody within three hundred miles of Greenwood has heard of Fairfax,' said the gunsmith. 'He owns most of the county from what I hear. Powerful man. I also hear it don't pay to cross him. Puttin' up for State Governor later in the year. So far there ain't nobody else against him nor likely to be from what I hear.'

'That sounds like the kind of thing Fairfax would do,' said Billy. 'I'm only surprised he waited so long.'

'You know Fairfax then?' asked the gunsmith.

'I know Fairfax,' Billy nodded, 'an' Fairfax knows me. He probably wishes he didn't know me but he does. I wouldn't bet on him still bein' around to take up that job of State Governor though.'

'That sounds like fightin' talk,' said the gunsmith. 'It could also explain why there were a couple of fellers through here some time ago. I overheard them talkin' about some feller called Billy Nesbitt and how they had to stop him reaching Greenwood. You're Billy Nesbitt, aren't you?'

'One and the same,' said Billy. 'Those two didn't stop me an' neither did two others before them. Like I say, don't put your money on Fairfax ever makin' governor.'

# 7

Before setting out again, Billy was assured that even riding his donkey, he should reach Greenwood in about two weeks. All he had to do was keep heading north. The one problem he might encounter was a narrow but high range of mountains about halfway — something he had already been made aware of. He was also told that it was quite possible that there could be snow, but that it should be higher up and that it should not be too thick at this time of year.

Billy had expected trouble but there had been no sign of anyone in the town. This absence made him wonder if anybody would be waiting for him along the road. Whatever happened, he would be prepared for it.

Apparently there was no other town before Greenwood, although there were a few farms, homesteads and a way-station for a stagecoach company, which also doubled as a trading post. The way-station was before the mountains. He was warned that the man who ran the way-station was not to be trusted and was always looking for ways to relieve travellers of their money. It was also rumoured that he was not above murdering lone travellers for little more than their horses and the clothes they wore.

He reached the foothills and the way-station on the afternoon of his eighth day out. During that time he had seen two farms and had purchased meat, cheese and bread from the second. As far as he could tell they had not overcharged him, something he found slightly unusual. It appeared that most homesteaders and farmers were only too keen to sell at inflated prices.

Bearing in mind the warning that the owner of the way-station was not a man to be trusted and since he was not looking for problems, Billy looked for a way of bypassing it. However, actual avoidance was impossible since it was situated at the head of a valley through which he had to pass, which meant, apart from climbing up the steep sides, he had to at least pass through the place. Since he was not in desperate need of supplies, he opted to ride straight through.

As he slowly rode past, he was acutely aware that he was being watched although he could not actually see anyone. Apart from a few horses in a paddock — obviously stagecoach company animals — about half a dozen pigs, three cows, a few hens, geese and ducks, there was no sign of life. He simply knew that his progress was being monitored very closely. He could almost feel the eyes boring into him. However, he was allowed to ride through unchallenged.

His journey through the mountains was cold and windy but otherwise uneventful. The road was plainly well used and the going easy. There was some snow, something he had not seen since his youth, but it presented no problems. Most of it was much higher up. However, Sam found a patch and seemed very puzzled. After leaping into it and emerging looking most surprised, he spent some time barking at it. A day later Billy found himself on the other side of the mountains and overlooking a wide, flat plain.

He felt a sense of relief course through his body and mind. He was almost at his destination and the fulfilment of many years of dreaming and planning. However, he realized that all the dreaming and planning of the past thirty years now counted for nothing. This was reality. Dreams and reality were far apart.

He had barely set foot on level ground when he heard the rumble of wheels behind him. A short time later a stagecoach passed him by. It appeared to have travelled over the mountains and so must have called in at the way-station. The driver and two passengers gave him strange looks as they drove past, the driver apparently taking the most interest in him. Billy put this down to the fact that it was not too often anyone came across a man and a dog riding a donkey. He did not give the matter another thought.

A short time later Billy came across a small farm-house where he called in just to make certain that he was on the right road for Greenwood. At first the elderly man and his wife looked at him strangely. They obviously had something on their mind. After being assured that he was on the right road, the man suddenly asked him if his name was Billy Nesbitt. The question took Billy by surprise.

'Might be,' he said. 'Who wants to know an' if it is, how did you know?'

'Mr Fairfax wants to know,' replied the man. 'Most the folk in these parts have been told to keep an eye open for you. We're supposed to let Fairfax know the moment you do come.'

'And are you goin' to let him know?' asked Billy.

'No, sir,' replied the man. 'I don't suppose you remember me, but me an' your pa were good friends. I used to live closer to Greenwood in those days. Fairfax bought me an' a few others out an' we had to move. I chose this place. Last time I saw you was at your trial. Never thought I'd see you alive again. Thirty years is a long time to survive prison and Fairfax was always goin' on about how few men lived long enough. The name's Flint, Joshua Flint.' Billy had to confess that the name meant nothing to him.

'From the way you're talkin' about Fairfax I'd say you don't have much time for him,' said Billy.

'That's 'cos we don't,' interrupted Mrs Flint. 'We didn't want to sell up but Fairfax made it impossible for us. Oh, it was all legal like, we did check that much. Sure, he paid us for our land, but not what it was really worth. I suppose we could've held out but the few who did try that suddenly found they couldn't sell their crops nowhere, couldn't pay their mortgage and the bank foreclosed. Most other folk were in the same position as well. No, sir, James Fairfax ain't exactly what you'd call a popular figure in these parts.'

'Most folk never believed that you murdered his father an' brother either,' said Joshua. 'We never knew for sure who did do it, but we all knew as sure as hell it wasn't you. It wasn't you, was it?'

'No,' said Billy. 'It wasn't me but I know who it was, I saw what happened.'

'You always said it was Fairfax himself,' said Joshua.

'An' that's exactly who it was,' said Billy. 'You say everybody knew I was innocent, but those twelve men of the jury *all* found me guilty.'

'That's 'cos they were all either selected by Fairfax or were in his pay in some way. It's a strange fact but them twelve men or their families are the only ones who still have land in Greenwood.

Most others, like me, have been either forced out or bought out by Fairfax for a pittance.'

'Whatever you've got in mind for that son-of-a-bitch is fine by us,' said Mrs Flint. 'Only wish there was some way we could help.'

'There's nothin' you can do,' said Billy. 'This is between me an' James Fairfax. Anyhow, I think he knows by now that I'm on my way, that I've made it this far. He's tried to have me stopped before but it didn't work. If you knew that I might be headin' this way, I reckon the man who runs the way-station on the other side of the mountains knows as well. He saw me pass through an' there's been a stage through since I was there. It wasn't that long ago, you must've seen it. He probably told the driver to tell Fairfax.'

'Nothin' more certain,' said Joshua. 'Fairfax owns the stagecoach company among other things. In fact there isn't much in the whole county and even beyond that he doesn't either own or have part shares in.'

'Not bad for a man whose father owned only a thousand acres,' mused Billy. 'Him an' my pa had the same size holdin'. I presume Fairfax bought out what should have been my land when my pa died? I know my pa died not long after I was sent to prison.'

'It wasn't that long after,' said Joshua. 'Your pa had an accident, which we all thought was kind of suspicious an' your ma didn't last long after he died. You might not remember her too well, but she always was a sickly woman.'

'Then this is for my ma an' pa as well,' said Billy.

★   ★   ★

Billy sat on top of a small hill simply staring down. From where he was he had a good view of the town of Greenwood straddling the river. To his right, about two miles from the town, he could see a large, white building which he assumed to be the ranch house belonging to James Fairfax. He also dug deep into his memory and finally located what he thought had been his home. From his viewpoint it appeared to be derelict. He was not too surprised.

He was in no hurry. Time was something he had long since learned how to deal with. He had become an expert at biding his time and had developed an ability to simply close down his mind and even body to allow time to pass unnoticed.

He knew that by now Fairfax would have been told that he was in the county and he hoped that he was sweating, wondering what was going to happen.

He wanted James Fairfax to sweat, he wanted him to know fear. He had also decided that one good way of instilling fear in Fairfax was for him, Billy, to do absolutely nothing of a threatening nature. He felt that his simply being there was menacing enough for the time being. At that moment he did not want to give James Fairfax any excuse at all to have him arrested or even killed.

Billy spent the whole day and all that night on that hill. By the morning he had only got as far as making up his mind to go into the town. If he came face to face with his adversary, so be it. He had no immediate plans to confront Fairfax, he would wait for James Fairfax to either find him or confront him. He wanted Fairfax to force the issue. He wanted Fairfax to appear the aggressor. He smiled to himself as he realized that what he really wanted was for James Fairfax to give him, Billy, a legal reason to kill him.

His arrival in Greenwood certainly caused a stir and Billy knew that his progress had been witnessed long before he reached the town. It was as if the whole town had turned out to see him. The fact that he had a dog riding with him and that he was riding a donkey caused very little comment.

Most people kept a respectful distance from him, although a few of the older residents did acknowledge him and he felt that he ought to remember some of them, but he did not. Those of his own age or younger were too young to really know who he was other than through what they had been told. After hitching his donkey and watching Sam run off to investigate, his first call was to the saloon. A place he had never been allowed inside as a youth.

'Beer,' he said, looking round at the almost empty room. He noted many faces peering through the windows and smiled to himself. 'You'd better tell them they're wastin' their time,' he said nodding at the windows. 'I ain't here to cause no trouble. I've been on the road a long time an' all I need right now is a drink,'

'You're Billy Nesbitt, ain't you?' said the bartender. Billy simply nodded. 'The whole town's heard about you. Most folk are surprised you made it this far. The bettin' was that you'd have an accident on the way.'

'I didn't,' said Billy. 'Four of Fairfax's men did though. Speakin' of bullshit, which I guess we weren't, where is Fairfax? I was kind of hopin' he might mount a reception committee.'

'Don't rightly know,' said the bartender. 'I ain't exactly in his confidence.'

'I'll bet you're in his pay though.'

'If you mean he owns this saloon, then I am in his pay,' agreed the bartender. 'That goes for the livery stable and the corn and seed merchants store as well.'

'But I'm not in his pay,' boomed a voice by the door. 'Sheriff Henry Fielding,' he continued by way of introduction. 'You probably believe Mr Fairfax owns everythin' and everybody in Greenwood, which he very nearly does. Just for the record though, he don't own me. You're Mr Billy Nesbitt I presume? As you probably saw by all the folk out on the street, you weren't unexpected.'

'The same,' nodded Billy, turning

slightly towards the sheriff. 'I suppose you've been sent to tell me to get my ass out of town?'

'Somethin' like that,' agreed the sheriff, standing alongside Billy and taking the beer placed in front of him. Billy noted that the sheriff paid for the drink. 'Leastways that's what Mr Fairfax would like me to tell you,' he continued, 'but like I say, I ain't in his pay. Never have been, never will be. What I will say though is that I run a good, clean town. I don't take no trouble from nobody, includin' James Fairfax and his men an' that's the way I intend to keep it.'

'Glad to hear it,' said Billy. 'You expectin' me to cause trouble? I expect Fairfax has told you I'm here to kill him.'

'I don't know you, Mr Nesbitt,' said the sheriff. 'There's a good many folk in these parts who do remember what happened between you an' Mr Fairfax.'

'Good many?' interrupted Billy. 'I heard that most folk who owned land had been moved out by Fairfax, by fair means or foul.'

'That was all before my time,' said the sheriff. 'The point is, the story of how you killed his father an' brother is common knowledge. It always was, but since the news that you'd been released from prison got out, there's been talk of nothin' else. Mainly about how you're hell-bent on revenge, on killin' Fairfax.'

'Hell-bent on revenge!' said Billy. 'I don't ever remember sayin' that to nobody. I ain't threatened Fairfax with nothin'. Is that why he appears to be out of town? I was kinda hopin' he'd be here to meet me. We have a lot to talk about.'

'He's around somewhere,' said the sheriff. 'Just take my advice an' get on your way an' forget about him.'

'Or else?' asked Billy.

'Or else I can't be responsible for what happens,' said the sheriff.

'But you're the law round here,' said Billy. 'You don't take no trouble off nobody including Fairfax. You just told me so yourself. What could possibly happen to me?'

'That all depends on you,' said the sheriff.

Having had his beer and, he felt, made a point, Billy took his donkey and headed for the cemetery where he assumed his mother and father would be buried. He was certainly not a religious man, but he felt that he ought to at least pay his respects to the memory of his father and mother.

He was met by the local minister who, after some thought, directed Billy to a corner of the burial ground where he assured Billy he would find the graves. To his credit, the minister did not ask Billy any questions.

Billy eventually found what he thought were the graves, now hardly discernible by almost thirty years of neglect. The only indications were two slight humps in the ground and two old, wooden crosses now lying alongside each grave. He picked up the crosses and took them to the minister, admitting that he could not read. The minister confirmed that the name burned into each cross was *Nesbitt*.

Billy spent some time tidying up each grave and replacing the crosses. All the time he was talking to both his parents, telling them that time for justice to be finally done was close at hand. Just as he had replaced the cross on his mother's grave, Sam turned up.

It was almost as if the dog sensed that this was something of a special occasion and he kept very quiet. Finally, Billy scratched the dog's head and said they were going to spend the night in the house where he was born.

Billy found that he was able to go straight to the house and, as he had expected, it was the one he had seen from the hill and there was not much left of it. He dragged some old timbers round the stone fireplace — which was still standing intact — made a crude shelter, lit a fire and cooked a meal for himself and Sam. Then he settled down for the night.

There was no need for Sam to alert him, he heard the horses at almost the same time as his dog. Even so, Sam growled and disappeared. Four riders slowly made their way towards him.

'You're on private property,' said one of the men. 'Mr Fairfax don't like trespassers on his land.'

'This land belonged to my father long before it belonged to Fairfax,' said Billy. 'I was born in this house.'

'Don't know nothin' about that,' grunted the man. 'All I know is it belongs to Mr Fairfax now.'

'And he sent you to get me off,' sneered Billy. 'Just like he sent those other men to make sure I never reached Greenwood. Well they didn't stop me, I'm here an' I guess Fairfax knows it. Pity he didn't come himself. We ain't seen each other for more'n thirty years. We've got a lot to talk about.'

'Mr Fairfax ain't got time to bother about scum like you,' said the man.

'So he sends other scum to do his dirty work,' goaded Billy. 'OK, I guess he legally owns this place now. I'll be off later on, when I'm ready.'

'Now!' grated the man.

'Now!' said Billy with a wry smile. 'So what happens if I choose not to go *now*? What happens if I decided not to go at all?'

'I don't think you understand,' hissed the man, slouching in his saddle. 'When I say *now* I mean *now*, this very second. If you don't, there's four guns against you. I don't know or care how you made it this far, but unless you get your ass off this land right now the only place you'll be goin' is under about six foot of dirt.'

Billy had not put on his gun and he stretched out his arms to show that he was unarmed.

'You'd shoot an unarmed man?' he challenged. 'OK, go ahead. That's just what Fairfax would want you to do. Only thing is, it'd be murder an' are you prepared to hang for somethin' which really ain't got nothin' to do with you? I know I was sent to prison for murder, he's probably told you I was supposed to have murdered his pa an' brother, but I was only sixteen at the time. Had I been any older they would have hanged me. I've seen lots of men hanged an' it ain't a pretty sight. Most don't die straight away, somebody usually has to swing on their legs until they choke to death.'

'There's no witnesses,' sneered the man. 'We could claim it was self-defence. Either way, it wouldn't matter to you, you'd be dead.'

'But it would matter to *me*,' a voice suddenly called out. They all turned to see Sheriff Henry Fielding standing by a tree about twenty yards way. 'Get the hell out of here, Mick Walker. I've seen an' heard enough to know that if anything happens to Nesbitt I'll have enough evidence to charge somebody with murder. OK, so he's trespassing, but this place doesn't feature very high on Fairfax's list does it? I'll bet Fairfax has even forgotten the place ever existed.'

The four men looked at each other and then, at a nod from Mick Walker, they turned and galloped off. Billy and the sheriff watched them disappear and then the sheriff went across to Billy.

'Nice timin',' said Billy.

'Not really,' said the sheriff. 'I saw them ride out of town and it was common knowledge that you'd come out here. It's damned hard to keep a secret in Greenwood. Sometimes it's like a man can't even fart in private without the whole town knowing about it. Anyhow, I guessed they were out to cause trouble so I followed. Maybe it's as well I did. Mick Walker is Fairfax's main gunman. If there's any dirty work needs doing, he sends Walker.'

'I would have thought having a man like that was not a good advertisement for a potential State Governor,' said Billy.

'You know about that?' said the sheriff. 'I've seen a few men go for high, political office and they all had men like Walker behind them somewhere.

Nobody takes much notice of things like that. I don't think you'll get much trouble from them again, at least not out here.'

'No, I guess that was just an opening gambit,' said Billy.

'Gambit?' queried the sheriff. 'For a man who can't even read that's strange word to use.'

'Just because I can't read or write don't make me stupid,' said Billy. 'It's a term used in chess. Strangely enough, I am a very good chess player. I learned to play the game in prison. I had a good teacher, a man who had had plenty of schoolin'. He was goin' to teach me how to read an' write but then he upped an' died on me. He was doin' life for murderin' his wife an' her lover. He'd only done three months when he got sick. He taught me the basics of chess and I taught myself the rest. It's a game that needs patience and cunning and I've got plenty of both.'

'Just watch out,' warned the sheriff. 'I won't always be around to protect you and I won't want to be either. If you have a grudge against Fairfax just make sure you keep it all legal. I hope I make myself plain. Don't worry, I've already told Fairfax the same thing.'

The sheriff returned to his horse which was some distance away and immediately Sam appeared. Billy teased him for being a coward, but he knew that his little friend was anything but.

With little else to do, Billy decided to leave his donkey and walk into town. He quite deliberately did not put on his gun and hid his belongings. He tried telling Sam to stay but Sam obviously had other ideas. Both walked slowly into town where he was met with curious looks and most folk crossed the street, probably fearing that trouble was not too far away.

'Glad to see you've decided to leave your guns off,' said the sheriff as Billy walked past his office. 'Maybe I shouldn't say this, but you are taking a bit of a risk. Mick Walker doesn't worry too much about things like that.'

'Then you'll have the perfect excuse to arrest him,' said Billy with a wry smile. 'I'm not too bothered, I don't think Fairfax can afford to get himself involved in murder. I notice he still hasn't shown his face. He must be scared.'

The sheriff nodded. 'You've got a point. In fact I have never seen him so worried. I saw him not long ago, out at his place. He told me to get you out of town. He says he doesn't want any trouble. What's done is done and nothing can change it. I must say I'm inclined to agree with him.'

'Justice hasn't been done,' said Billy. 'I had to serve thirty years for somethin' I didn't do. All I want is justice. I'll be in the saloon if he wants me.'

'Just remember,' warned the sheriff, 'justice doesn't mean murder.'

It was too early for most of the citizens of Greenwood to be drinking, although once again there were several faces peering through the windows as he ordered a beer. He had been there for about ten minutes when a buzz of excitement could be heard. Billy turned his back on the door but watched what was happening in the reflection of a large mirror.

Mick Walker and his three companions burst into the room and immediately the only two other people in the saloon decided that they had more pressing matters to attend. Billy kept an eye on the four men but did not turn round.

'You ain't welcome in here,' barked Walker. 'Mr Fairfax has decided that you can't be served. Get your ass outside.'

Billy deliberately looked about the room before looking at the four men. 'You talkin' to me?' he asked.

'Since you're the only one in here, I must be,' rasped Walker. 'You're banned from this saloon an' since there ain't no other, I guess that means you can't drink nowheres.'

Billy looked Walker up and down for

a moment and then laughed. 'You're a big man against a man who ain't armed,' he said. 'How do you fancy your chances in a fist fight? I reckon I could take the four of you on, no problem at all.'

Walker appeared rather uncertain and fingered the handle of his gun. Billy laughed again and decided that the time was not quite right to force the issue. He drained his glass and pushed past the four men. Outside, he met a relieved looking sheriff but a disappointed crowd.

# 8

Nothing much happened for the next two days and Billy continued to live in the remains of his old house. During that time there was neither sight nor sound of James Fairfax, although Billy was assured that he was around — somewhere. Nor was there any sign of Mick Walker. It appeared that he had been warned off for the moment. Billy continued to use the saloon, at first more as an act of defiance than anything else. The bartender had obviously been uncertain as to what to do but in the absence of instructions to the contrary, decided he had better serve him. He had also decided not to chance incurring Billy's wrath.

On the morning of the third day, however, there was a flurry of activity when a stagecoach arrived. It's occupants were five men, three of whom, it was plain even to Billy, were very important people judging by their manner and dress. The other two were not quite so well dressed and appeared to be tolerated by the other three rather than treated as equals. One thing was quite clear though, they were not servants or employees. Even though the other two were apparently lesser beings, the three important men treated them with some deference. For the first time Billy saw James Fairfax, who had obviously come into town to meet the stage. The status of the party was confirmed when the three important men were introduced to Fairfax and shook hands whilst the other two simply received curt nods.

Had he not been told that this was James Fairfax, Billy would not have recognized him. The tall, thin young man from thirty years previously had been replaced by a still tall but now rather portly man sporting a pointed beard and who appeared to walk with a limp. He seemed to know who Billy was and for a few moments both men eyed each other from a distance, but neither made any move or said anything. Billy, for his part, was content to wait.

The information circulating was that the three men were from the State Capital and had come to help launch James Fairfax's campaign to become governor and the other two were newspaper men. At first they were all taken off to Fairfax's ranch, but Billy learned that they were coming back that afternoon. A public meeting was to be held and due to take place in the only place expected to be large enough to accommodate a crowd — the saloon.

Billy decided to attend the meeting, although he was not strictly speaking concerned with the campaign. As far as he was aware he was not one of the electorate. That point did not bother Billy, his only reason for attending the meeting was to hopefully make things uncomfortable for Fairfax. In that respect it appeared that he had already been successful. His presence had obviously come at an inopportune time for James Fairfax.

Billy had positioned himself by the door and when Fairfax entered the room in the company of the others, his presence was obvious to all, particularly Fairfax who had to brush past him. For a brief moment both men stared at each other and Billy's presence plainly annoyed Fairfax. It seemed as if Fairfax was going to object to Billy being there as he made to speak to the sheriff, but then he apparently decided not to pursue the matter.

There were about a hundred people in the room — all men. No self-respecting woman from Greenwood would set foot in such a place, even if it was being used for political purposes. Eventually, when Fairfax and the other three were seated and supplied with drinks, the meeting was called to order.

Billy listened patiently while one of the visitors droned on about how lucky the people of Greenwood were to have such a noble and sincere man who was prepared to take on the office of governor. When he finally ended his speech, James Fairfax stood up and too droned on about how he was so well suited for the position. Eventually Billy could take no more and felt compelled to speak.

'I guess it won't make much difference either way what I have to say,' he said. 'I hear that nobody else is puttin' up for the job . . . '

'Not quite right,' interrupted the first speaker. 'Until three days ago there had been no other candidates, but when nominations finally closed, two more names had been put forward. There are now three candidates for the position, which means that every vote counts, including yours . . . '

'Don't count me,' said Billy. 'I don't rightly know if I'm entitled to the vote or even where. Mr Fairfax knows that better'n most. I've just spent the last thirty years in prison for murder, murders which Fairfax knows I didn't commit.' There was a general murmur round the room and all eyes were now on Billy. Fairfax was plainly very uncomfortable. 'The name is Billy Nesbitt,' continued Billy, 'an' I was convicted of murderin' his father an' brother. Ask him, he'll tell you all about it.'

The man coughed and glanced nervously at Fairfax. 'It is well known what happened to Mr Fairfax's father and brother,' he said. 'If you *are* who you say you are, then you must know that you received a fair trial. At least you didn't hang for what you did. However, that is now all in the past and has no bearing on Mr Fairfax's bid to become governor of the state. Unless you have a question or observation regarding his election, I must ask you to keep quiet.'

'I ain't got no interest in politics,' said Billy. 'In fact I don't reckon most folk got that much interest. All politicians are good for is talkin'. We used to get them lookin' round the prison from time to time. Didn't make no difference though, nothin' ever changed, at least not for the better. I'd just like the folk of Greenwood to know that the man before them, claimin' such high ideals, is a murderer, that's all. He murdered his own father an' brother. It wasn't me. He just made sure it was me what got the blame. I did thirty years in hell on account of that man's lies.'

Everyone in the room tried to talk at once and the two newspaper men were writing furiously. Billy suddenly found that Sheriff Henry Fielding had taken his arm and was ushering him out of the door. He did not resist, he felt quite pleased that he had made his point and even more pleased that it had been in the presence of distinguished company and the newspaper men.

'I think there's laws against you saying what you said,' the sheriff said once they were outside. 'You can't just go round claiming somebody is a murderer without proof.'

'So arrest me,' invited Billy. 'It might

be a good thing. I can then tell the truth in court.'

'That's up to Mr Fairfax,' said the sheriff. 'All I can say is if you do have proof then take the matter up legally.'

'Only proof I have is what I saw with my own eyes,' said Billy. 'I saw Fairfax shoot his own father an' brother.'

'It was all before my time,' said the sheriff, 'but I have been doing some checking and you made that claim at your trial. It wasn't good enough then, so I'm quite sure it isn't good enough now. I'm goin' to lock you up while I sort things out.' Once again, Billy did not object as he was led away to the jail.

It was about an hour later when James Fairfax entered the sheriff's office. He asked the sheriff to leave while he talked to Billy. The sheriff was uncertain but when Billy said that it was all right as far as he was concerned, he agreed. When they were alone, Billy and Fairfax stared coldly at each other for a couple of minutes.

'It won't do you any good,' Fairfax

suddenly said. 'You were found guilty of those murders, not me. As far as the law is concerned you are the murderer, not me.' He looked Billy up and down and smiled. 'You always were a big lad. Big, simple and dangerous, that's what we used to say. Useless at most things except when it came to using your brawn or your fists. You were a good fighter even then. I hear you've made a habit of fighting for money. Did you ever learn to read and write? You couldn't all those years ago.'

'No, never did,' admitted Billy. 'They didn't have many readin' classes in Sonora. I can play chess though. Can you play chess, Jimmy? Patience an' cunning, that's what chess is all about. It's about gettin' your opponent tied up so's no matter what, he can't move nowhere without dyin'. I had me a long time to learn about patience an' cunning. A man needs those things an' more to survive the system in prison.'

'I play chess,' said Fairfax. 'I'm surprised you can. I would have thought it too complicated for your simple mind to cope with. What you said in the saloon just now wasn't wise. I believe there are laws about what's known as slander. However, in this case I do not consider it to be in either your interest or mine to pursue the matter. I don't intend bringing any charges. My advice to you is get the hell out of this county and this state while you still can.'

'More threats, Jimmy?' sneered Billy. 'It was you who made the first moves in this game. It was you who sent those two out to Sonora to kill me. It was you who sent the other two just in case they failed. Well they all failed, didn't they? You even tried to get Mick Walker to kill me but he failed as well. So far it looks like I play chess better'n you, don't it? I hear there's two newspaper men with you from important newspapers so I can see why you want me out of the way. You don't want me talkin' too much just in case the truth comes out. You owe me, Jimmy, you owe me thirty years of my life. At least *we* both know the truth of it, that's all that matters as far as I'm concerned. It could be bad for you if the big newspapers start runnin' with this thing.'

'You couldn't prove a thing then and you can't prove a thing now, Nesbitt,' said Fairfax. 'Sure, you might make life a bit difficult for me, but it won't last. You'll be seen for what you are, an oaf with a grudge.'

'I still reckon I can play chess better'n you,' said Billy.

'You've had a run of good luck, that's all,' said Fairfax. 'OK, as far as I'm concerned you are free to go. Just remember, back in Sonora you were on what you might call home territory. This is my territory now and I make the rules. If you want to stay alive I suggest you get the hell out of it while you can.'

'Is that another threat, Jimmy?' said Billy with a wry laugh. 'I do believe it was.' He called out for the sheriff and when he came through Billy laughed again. 'OK, Jimmy, tell the sheriff what you told me. He threatened to have me killed, Sheriff. That's right, Jimmy, ain't it?'

'It's *Mr Fairfax* to you, Nesbitt,' growled Fairfax. 'I didn't threaten you with anything. Just get him out of my hair and out of this territory, Sheriff. He's liable to do himself some damage if he stays around.'

'If you say so, Mr Fairfax,' said the sheriff. 'You're not taking what he said any further?'

'I don't have the time and he's just not worth the bother,' snarled Fairfax as he stormed out.

However it appeared that the two newspaper men were very interested in Billy. They were waiting for him outside the jail.

'Mr Billy Nesbitt,' said the one. 'We'd like to talk to you. Can we buy you a drink and have a talk in the saloon?'

'Why not,' said Billy. 'I guess it won't make any difference as to what happens to me. Leastways not if Jimmy Fairfax has his way.'

'Meaning what, exactly?' asked one of them as they led Billy away.

For the next two hours Billy was kept well supplied with beer and the newspaper men used up a lot of note paper.

That evening, Mick Walker and his three companions suddenly reappeared. They found Billy in the process of cooking his evening meal. Their arrival had not taken Billy by surprise — Sam had alerted him long before the men arrived.

'I was wonderin' when you'd turn up,' said Billy. 'I suppose you've come to warn me off, maybe even to force me into doin' somethin' stupid so you can have an excuse to kill me. Well take a good look, I ain't armed.'

'You've been talkin' to those newspaper men,' snarled Walker. 'Mr Fairfax don't like it when you talk to men like that, especially when it's all lies.'

'Lies!' said Billy with a wry laugh.

'What would you know about it? It was me who was there, not you.'

'Lies,' repeated Walker. 'The thing is them newspaper men have been sendin' off wires to their papers. Tellin' them lies ain't nice. Mr Fairfax wants you to make it plain to them that what you said was all lies. Now he says to tell you that he's a reasonable man an' he appreciates that you've just spent the last thirty years in prison. So, to show there's no hard feelin', he's prepared to make you an offer to pay you. He reckons two hundred dollars should be about right. He pays you an' you get the hell out of here.'

'An' you can tell him to go shit on his money,' snarled Billy. 'I was born here, I got some right to be here an' I got even more right to see that he pays for what he did to me.'

'Mr Fairfax will be very sorry you think like that,' said Walker. 'You know he's puttin' for governor, he can't allow scum like to you spoil his chances.'

'Can't allow!' exclaimed Billy. 'I

193

don't give a damn what he can or can't allow. What's he goin' to do, get you to kill me?'

'Could be,' said Walker. 'Think about it, Nesbitt. Two hundred dollars is a lot of money to a man like you. It's a lot of money to most folk. Take my advice, accept the money an' forget about it.'

'You can go shit as well,' snapped Billy. 'One way or another Jimmy Fairfax is goin' to pay for the last thirty years.'

Walker laughed and the men turned their horses and rode off. Half an hour later Sheriff Fielding arrived. His main concern was to check that Billy was still alive. He had seen Walker coming back and had feared the worst. He did not lecture Billy about the futility of his mission, but he did confirm that the newspaper men had sent off long messages to their respective papers reporting Billy's allegations. Billy was well pleased. In fact he was so pleased he decided to have a celebratory drink. The saloon was full but the moment

194

Billy entered all talking ceased and everyone eyed him with interest. The two newspaper men were seated at a table and called Billy over. A drink was brought to him and slowly people started talking again. It was very obvious what the subject of conversation was.

'I hear tell you've sent a report to your papers.' said Billy. 'Fairfax sent his man, Mick Walker to warn me off. He wanted me to say that it was all lies. He even offered me two hundred dollars if I did.'

'Too late for that now,' said one of them. 'The story will be in all editions first thing in the morning.'

'Doesn't it bother you that it might not be the truth?' asked Billy.

'We made it plain it was an allegation by you, not us,' said the other man. 'Anyhow, it is the truth, isn't it? We've been doing some checking on you as well and it appears you are who you claim to be. We also managed to get hold of a transcript of your trial and it makes for very interesting reading. Personally, I believe you *are* telling the truth.'

'I ain't got nothin' to gain by tellin' lies,' said Billy with a grin. 'If you want to know more, I suggest you hang about. I think things are about to happen.'

'We're supposed to leave in the mornin',' said one. 'I know one thing, the political group Fairfax is standing for are beginning to have second thoughts. The word is that he is about to be dropped.'

'Then they must think there's something in it,' said Billy.

'Not necessarily,' said the other man. 'They just can't afford to be seen to be behind a man whose integrity is in question. Politics is a funny business and most of them have something to hide in their past but they can't afford to lay themselves open to even the suggestion of dishonesty, and certainly not the question of his being a murderer. Whatever the truth of it all might be, I'd say you've just success-fully destroyed his political career. As I say, we did check on you and your background before we sent our stories off. You checked out fine and talking to folk who were around at the time, all thought you had been wrongly accused. We even found one old man who claims he was bribed by Fairfax to find you guilty. He says most of the other jurors were also bribed in one way or another.'

'Just check on how many of them were never bought out or forced off their land,' said Billy. 'That should tell you somethin'.'

Billy had been surprised that there had been no sign of Mick Walker during the evening. At the very least he had expected to be told that he was barred from the saloon. The newspaper men retired about an hour after Billy had arrived, but from then on it seemed that nobody was going to chance the wrath of James Fairfax by being seen talking to him. He too finally called it a day shortly before midnight. As ever, Sam was waiting outside for him.

The walk back to the old farm house was the best part of a mile and he and Sam had walked most of it without any bother. They were about a hundred yards away when Sam suddenly growled. Billy was immediately on his guard.

They were approaching a clump of trees when Sam growled once again and ran off in the direction of the trees. There was a moon which gave sufficient light to enable Billy to see enough and, as he approached the trees, he was aware of at least two figures. He needed no telling as to who they were.

'I know you're there, Walker,' Billy called.

'Sure, we're here,' a voice replied. 'There's two of us in front of you an' two behind. I hear you're a good fighter, Nesbitt. Reckon you can handle four of us? You ain't got no sheriff nor no newspaper men lookin' after you now.'

'I don't need no nursemaidin',' replied Billy.

Suddenly Sam raced past him, barking loudly and Billy turned to see two figures rapidly closing in on him. He dodged two blows, took a third on his chest, which had little effect, and his fist slammed into something bony which proved to be a face. The man collapsed in a heap but by that time the other two had closed in from the front.

Billy took two painful blows, neither of which were made by bare fists. They were definitely more like rifle butts. As tough as Billy might have been, even he was no match for sustained blows by rifle butts and they were enough to put him on the ground. Immediately he was surrounded and boots and rifle butts were crashing into his body. He managed to grab at least two boots and the wearers were sent to the ground. That gave him enough time to get to his feet and his fist crashed into the soft belly of one of the men.

'Come on, Walker!' gasped Billy.

'There's four of you, you can do better'n that, can't you.'

'An' there's two of you,' rasped a voice. 'You an' that damned dog. He's bitten me twice already.'

'He ain't fussy who he bites,' said Billy, riding a blow. His fist once again slammed into the softer parts of one of his assailants.

However, both Billy and Sam were no match for four men wielding rifles and one particular savage blow sent Billy crashing to the ground. Once again boots and butts crashed into his body. Then, quite suddenly, the assault ceased.

'That was just a sample of what will happen to you, Nesbitt,' said the familiar voice of James Fairfax. 'Thanks to you it looks as though my nomination for governor is to be withdrawn. I hope you're satisfied. However, it does have one good point: I am now free to deal with you as I like. The offer of two hundred dollars for your retraction no longer stands. On this occasion think yourself fortunate you got away with your life. Next time you might not be so lucky.'

'What you really mean is you can't afford for me to be killed,' croaked Billy. 'The sheriff ain't in your pay an' he knows all about you an' me.'

'Think what you like, Nesbitt,' said Fairfax with a wry laugh. 'If you know what's good for you, you'll get the hell out of here right now. You can give him another reminder,' he said to Walker. 'Just enough to let him know where he stands — or lies. Goodnight to you, Nesbitt. I do hope we never see each other again.'

Once again boots slammed into Billy's body and, when they had finished and were about to leave, Walker bent down and whispered in his ear.

'You're a dead man, Nesbitt,' he said. 'Once you're out of this county, ain't nobody goin' to care what happens to you.'

There was one more hard kick and Billy blacked out.

* ★ *

'He took a fair old beating,' said a disembodied voice somewhere above Billy's head.

'He might have a couple of cracked ribs, but nothing too serious. What happened?'

'I can guess,' said another voice. Billy struggled to bring voices and faces into focus. 'Mick Walker. Proving it is another matter though. Can you hear me, Nesbitt? Was it Mick Walker?'

'What do you think?' was what Billy wanted to say. Whether or not he succeeded he did not know. 'Where am I?'

'In jail,' replied the sheriff. 'Don't worry, you're not under arrest. There was nowhere else to bring you.'

Daylight shone through a window and Billy realized that he must have been unconscious for some time. 'How'd you find me?' he managed to ask.

'That dog of yours,' replied the

sheriff. 'He was waitin' for me when I opened the office. He was so darned insistent that I knew somethin' was wrong. I found you not far from your old house. It was Mick Walker, wasn't it?'

Billy nodded. 'Fairfax was there too,' he croaked. 'Can't say if he beat up on me or not, don't think so, but he was there all right.'

'I knew it,' said the sheriff. 'Only problem is it's your word against his and a few more. I've already questioned Fairfax and there are at least three reliable witnesses to say that he and Mick Walker were out at his ranch all night.'

'Very convenient,' said Billy. 'It don't matter though. I'll just add it to the list of what Jimmy Fairfax owes me. Where's Sam?'

'Sam?' asked the sheriff. 'Oh, you mean your dog. He's right here, under the bed. He refused to leave you.'

Billy dropped his hand and felt Sam lick it. He smiled. 'Thanks Sam,' he said. 'I guess I owe you again. Fairfax told me he was probably bein' withdrawn from the election. Is that right?'

'It certainly looks like it,' said the doctor, who was in the process of cleaning Billy's cuts and bruises. 'There was a telegraph message through to his lawyer this morning and according to the telegraph clerk he *is* finished. There won't be too many people crying about it, at least not in these parts. You probably guessed that he was not a popular man. In fact most people in Greenwood County would have voted for your donkey rather than him.'

'OK, Nesbitt,' said the sheriff. 'You've successfully destroyed his political career, I think you ought to be satisfied with that.'

'I'll think about it,' said Billy. 'Right now all I need is some rest.'

# 9

Billy refused to stay in the jail, claiming it brought back bitter memories of prison. When he felt a little better, he returned to his old house. Still feeling rather groggy, he lit a fire and very quickly fell asleep. The next time he awoke the fire was out and the position of the sun puzzled him, but eventually he realized that he must have been asleep for almost twenty-four hours.

It appeared that Sam had not moved from his side during all that time. When he had lain down, Sam had been curled up at his side and was still in exactly the same position when he woke. He patted the dog's head and announced that he now felt much better. Sam licked his hand and then trotted off out of sight.

For some time Billy thought about what had happened. The more he thought about it, the more he realized that his previous lust for blood had more-or-less disappeared.

He was surprised; if anyone had suggested to him even the day before, that he would lose the drive for vengeance, he would have been quite certain that nothing less than the dead body of James Fairfax would have satisfied him. Now, however, he even felt slightly sorry for the man. He was not *too* sorry though.

He was very pleased with the way things had turned out. James Fairfax had suffered what to him must have been a great humiliation. His political ambitions were now in tatters. His hopes of fame had been shattered by a man who could not even read or write and that was probably the greatest humiliation of all.

Billy recalled the words of those he now knew had been talking common sense all along. What had happened in the past had happened and no amount of further humiliation of or even the killing of Fairfax would alter a thing. In a peculiar way he even felt a sense of relief.

'Sam,' he said to the dog when it returned, 'I reckon we've been here long enough, don't you?' Sam wagged his tail. 'I guess that means you've had enough too. OK, what say we head back home?' Sam appeared to look questioningly at him and Billy laughed. 'Sure, that's what I said,' Billy continued. 'Back home. What home? That's what you're askin'. Well as far as I'm concerned that means goin' back to Mary an' Josh.' Sam's tail wagged again. 'OK, that's where we're goin'. I'll pick up a few supplies first an' tell the sheriff. I reckon he'll be pleased to see the back of me. I don't know if Fairfax will be pleased or not an' I don't care a damn.'

Sheriff Henry Fielding was indeed very pleased to hear that Billy had decided to call it a day. He said that he would pass on the news to James Fairfax. Billy had the impression that Fairfax would know all about it long before the sheriff told him. The unseen telegraph system was very efficient at such things.

The sheriff also confirmed that the political career of James Fairfax had indeed been ended. He had spoken to Fairfax not long before Billy had turned up and he had confirmed that his nomination had been withdrawn. The sheriff also warned Billy that because of the mood he was in, it would be better if he avoided both Fairfax and his men.

'You should be all right all the time you're in the county,' said the sheriff. 'What happens after that though, I can't vouch for. Just keep your eyes and ears open, that's all I can say. I don't *think* Fairfax will do anything stupid, but you never know. He was very bitter about you and said something about getting even. Have you got any particular place in mind to go?'

'Sure have,' said Billy. 'I hope you don't mind if I don't tell you though. I reckon it'd be better if nobody knows.'

'You're probably right,' agreed the

sheriff. 'Best of luck, Billy. You're doing the right thing in leaving now. If you'd stayed I don't think it would've been too long before either you or Fairfax was dead and the other under arrest for a murder which need never have happened.'

Billy bought enough supplies to last him on the journey back to the farm which, if he remembered correctly, would take at least four weeks, possibly five weeks. He was about to ride out when he suddenly became aware of somebody standing behind him.

He turned to see James Fairfax flanked by two of his men. Mick Walker was standing a few yards to one side. It appeared that he, Billy, was not going to be allowed to leave Greenwood in peace.

'Going somewhere, Nesbitt?' rasped Fairfax.

'I'm doin' what you told me to do an' gettin' my ass out of here,' replied Billy. 'I don't want to kill you no more, Jimmy.'

'*You* don't want to kill me!' snarled Fairfax. 'Well I've got news for you, *Nesbitt*, I sure as hell want to kill you. I suppose you're satisfied with ruining my career. Well I've got news for you, that was the worst thing you ever did.'

'Nearly as bad as you murderin' your own pa an' brother an' me bein' blamed for it?' asked Billy. 'I'd say it was a fair trade. Thirty years of my life for one ruined career in politics.'

'You're scum, Nesbitt,' snarled Fairfax. 'You always were nothing more than vermin and always will be. I kill vermin, Nesbitt. I shoot rats and rabbits and I squash cockroaches into the ground, just like I'm going to squash you.'

'Then maybe you'd better get on with it,' challenged Billy. 'It's four of you against one of me. I'd say they was just about the kind of odds you need.' He looked at Mick Walker and then at the other two men and smiled. 'OK, which one of you is goin' to kill me? Jimmy here won't, that's for sure. Why do you think he hires men like you? I'll tell you why. He don't want to get his hands dirty, he wants to be able to claim that it wasn't him who squeezed the trigger. It'll be one of you who ends up danglin' on the end of a rope, not him.'

'He's right!' Sheriff Henry Fielding stepped off the boardwalk and moved towards them. 'Nesbitt here has seen sense and decided to end the feud between him and you, Mr Fairfax. I suggest you take some of your own advice. What's happened has happened and there's nothing you can do about it now, except maybe make things worse for yourself.'

'*I* run this town, Fielding,' snapped Fairfax. 'I run it because I own most of it. I'm the real law, not you. If I say jump, folk round here only ask one question and that is, *how high, Mr Fairfax?* You're up for election soon and I'll make certain you don't get elected if you don't mind your own business. Now keep out of this and you just might keep your job.'

'Perhaps you can scare enough people into not voting for me again,' said the sheriff. 'Who are you going to put in my place, Walker here? You'd like that wouldn't you, Walker? You'd like to play the big man, ordering folk round, locking them in jail. I only hope Mr Fairfax pays you more than I get paid. Sure, you can see to it that I'm not elected again but until that election *I'm* the law. The only way you can change that is if you have me killed.'

'That can be arranged,' snarled Fairfax, 'and there's not a damned thing anybody can or will do about it. You're becoming a pain in the butt, Fielding. I want rid of you and I want rid of Nesbitt. I own this town and that makes me the law and nobody will argue with whatever I do.'

The nod from Fairfax was almost imperceptible and plainly missed by the sheriff, but it was not missed by Billy or Mick Walker.

Mick Walker had turned to face the

sheriff and suddenly he drew his pistol and fired. At the same time the gun in Billy's holster swivelled and it too blasted its deadly shot at Walker.

The sheriff fell to the ground and in the same instance Mick Walker, who had been no more than three yards from Billy, seemed to fly into the air and finally hit the ground at the feet of James Fairfax who simply stared in horror. Blood had splattered both him and the two men at his side.

'Who's next?' asked Billy, his gun now aimed at all three of them. 'That's a stupid question. From this distance one shot would take the three of you. Don't any of you move a muscle or you all die.'

By that time other people had rushed out on to the street, including the doctor who immediately ran to attend the sheriff. It seemed that he was not too badly injured, little more than a flesh wound in his upper chest. Mick Walker, on the other hand, was dead. His face had been blasted away.

'Nesbitt murdered him!' shouted Fairfax.

'I saw what happened, Mr Fairfax,' said the doctor, 'and it certainly wasn't murder. Walker drew his gun first and tried to shoot the sheriff.' At least three other people confirmed what the doctor claimed. 'Why would he try to kill the sheriff, Mr Fairfax?' he asked. 'That's not something a man like Walker would do on his own account.'

'I must ask the same question,' said the sheriff, standing up. 'It looks like your man got what was coming to him, thanks to Billy. In fact I'd go so far as to say Walker was acting on your orders, especially after our conversation. I reckon I'm only alive now because Nesbitt acted so quickly. I ought to slam you up in jail for attempted murder and I still might.'

'Prove it!' snapped Fairfax. 'And what conversation, Sheriff? Nesbitt murdered my father and brother and he murdered Mick Walker. Once a murderer, always a murderer.'

'You know I'll never be able to prove it,' said the sheriff. 'Just like I'll never be able to prove you threatened to have me replaced as sheriff. I'm beginning to wonder if there is any substance in what Nesbitt claims. In fact in a way it makes perfect sense.'

'Think what you like, Sheriff,' snarled Fairfax. 'That goes for the rest of you as well. Just remember I own most of you in one way or another. It's true, Nesbitt's wild claims mean that I am no longer in the running for governor. That's what you wanted wasn't it, Nesbitt? You came back here looking for what you claim was justice. Well you had your justice, you had thirty years in prison for murders the law said you committed.'

'Sure, that's what the law said,' agreed Billy, 'but you an' me both know the truth of it. I saw you shoot your pa an' your brother. Don't ask me why you should do such a thing, I just don't know, but shoot 'em you did. You saw me an' twisted things so that it looked

215

like I did it. I wasn't too good with words, I couldn't read or write, but you were always real clever at such things.' He looked at the people now gathered round and smiled thinly. 'That's what I told 'em at the trial an' that's what I'm tellin' you now. It's the truth. I couldn't prove nothin' then an' I can't prove nothin' now. I'm leavin', I decided he just ain't worth the bother no more. Nothin' I can do will bring back my thirty years.'

'I'll find you, Nesbitt,' snarled Fairfax. 'I don't care where you go, I'll find you and you'll pay for what you did to me.'

'Fair trade, I'd say,' said Billy with a broad grin.

A short time later he and Sam left Greenwood riding the donkey and, despite the shooting, there did not appear to be many people to witness his departure. As ever the donkey was slow and Billy resolved that at the earliest opportunity he would learn how to ride a horse.

For the first few days Billy was on constant lookout for signs of being followed. He had the feeling that one of Fairfax's men would follow just to see where he went. However, it seemed that he was wrong.

He passed the farm belonging to the Flints who came out to meet him. News that Fairfax was no longer in the running for governor had reached them and they appeared very pleased about it. Billy continued his slow progress and after five days was quite convinced that he was not being followed.

He had to admit to some surprise. He had been fully prepared to fight, although that was the last thing he now wanted. His lust for blood had been replaced with a strong desire to settle down with Mary Stanton and assume a normal, mundane life as a farmer. He still remembered what it was like to live on a farm and thought he knew enough to be able to pick up the threads once again.

It took him just over five weeks to

reach the farm and whilst Mary's father, Josh, did not seem at all surprised to see him, Mary herself was plainly, if pleasantly, surprised. He told them what had happened, that Fairfax was still alive and that even though he had not apparently been followed, he still would not be surprised if Fairfax did try to find him.

'I don't want to put either of you in danger,' he said. 'I'll move on if you want me to.'

'Now you know full well that's not what either of us want,' said Mary. 'OK, so if Fairfax does come after you there's not much we can do about it. We'll just have to manage as best we can.'

Billy smiled and looked round the small room. 'I reckon this place could do with bein' bigger,' he said. 'I had me some experience of buildin' while I was in prison. There's plenty of good rock round here, it shouldn't take me too long to build on to this lot.'

'I was thinkin' the same thing myself,' said Josh. 'A woman an' her man don't want other folk clutterin' up the place of a night. OK, Billy, you do what you've a mind to do. Just tell me what you want. In the meantime me an' Sam can sleep in the barn.'

'And what's all this about a woman and her man?' asked Mary, although there was a distinctly happy glint in her eye. 'Who might you be talkin' about?'

'I was thinkin' of movin' the widder Turner in here,' said her father. 'She allus said I only had to ask.'

'Over my dead body!' snapped Mary. 'You move in with her if you've a mind to, but she don't ever set one foot over *my* doorway. Anyhow, you've always said that she was the last person you'd ever want to live with.'

'Too darned right,' grunted Josh. 'That woman never gave her two husbands anythin' but a sore ear from all her natterin' an' naggin'. Married twice she was,' he explained to Billy. 'Never had no kids, allus said her men weren't up to it. Not up to it! She never stopped talkin' long enough for them to bed her, that's the truth of it. Who did you think I meant, my girl? Mind you, maybe Billy don't like the idea, nobody's asked him yet.'

'It isn't up to the woman to ask the man,' pointed Mary. 'I've managed this long without a man, I think I can last a lot longer.'

'It sounds like a good idea to me,' said Billy. 'That's if you'll have me, Mary?'

'Have you!' she squealed, throwing herself at him. 'You stupid great oaf, of course I will.' She gave him a long kiss, which clearly embarrassed him.

'There's just one thing,' he said, pushing away slightly. 'I was sixteen when I was sent to prison an' I was there for thirty years. I guess that makes me . . .'

'Forty-six,' said Mary.

'Sure, if you say so,' mumbled Billy, 'forty-six. I reckon I must be just about the only 46-year-old man in the whole of America who can't ride a horse, use a gun properly or who ain't never had himself a woman. In fact I ain't never even seen a woman naked.'

'Didn't you ever have a girl when you was a boy?' she asked. 'From what I hear these days most girls an' boys know what it's all about by the time they're sixteen.'

'Well, I didn't,' said Billy. 'I know some boys did, but I was never much with girls. Mostly they used to laugh at me. I saw some strange things goin' on in prison between men an' most of the other older prisoners allus wanted me to do the same thing with them. Never did though, just didn't seem natural to me an' I was allus big enough to make sure nobody never tried forcin' me into it.'

'Then I guess I'll just have to teach you all about it,' she whispered. 'I'd kinda like to be married though, but there ain't no preacher within a hundred miles of here as I know of.'

'Who needs a preacher?' asked Billy.

'I do!' she pouted.

As promised Josh moved out into the

barn, Billy and Mary took over the house and they all worked hard over the next four weeks extending it. Eventually it was twice the size it had been and two extra rooms were added.

During that time they had all kept a lookout for James Fairfax or anyone who looked as though they might be working for him, but apart from a couple of neighbours calling, there had been no sign of anyone. However, the day after the extension to the house had been completed, Josh suddenly rushed in and grabbed his shotgun.

'Somebody's comin',' he said breathlessly. 'Too far away to see who it is though, but it sure ain't nobody I know.'

'Just the one?' asked Billy.

'As far as I can see,' said Josh. 'Could be just a scout sent out by Fairfax though.'

'Then I don't think we're goin' to need guns,' said Billy. 'Even if it is one of Fairfax's men, he wouldn't be so stupid as to try anythin' on his own.'

'I'll take the gun just in case,' insisted Josh.

They all stood outside the house watching as a figure on horseback slowly made his way towards them. Suddenly Billy laughed.

'Looks like you got your preacher,' he said to Mary. 'That's Father Sean Ryan. He's a Catholic priest. I met him in Sonora.'

'Catholic!' said Mary. 'I'm not a Catholic. Are you?'

'I ain't nothin',' said Billy. 'Does it really matter what he is? As far as I know Catholic priests can still wed folk.'

'I suppose so,' said Mary, 'but Catholic! I've never met a Catholic priest.'

'Well there's always a first time,' said Billy. 'Don't worry, he's only human. He don't go round eatin' babies or anythin' like that.'

Eventually the figure arrived and for a moment he looked at Billy and then smiled.

'Well now, if it isn't Billy Nesbitt,' he said sliding off his horse. 'I never thought to see you again. There can't be much fightin' round these parts.'

'I've given that up,' said Billy, shaking the priest's hand. 'I never thought to meet you again either. Father, I want you to meet my new family. This is Mary and this is her father, Josh. You couldn't have come at a better time. Anyhow, what brings you out here?'

The priest shook hands with Josh and Mary and looked round at the house. 'Nice place you've got here. That bit looks new.' He pointed to the extension. 'Now I know this might sound a bit forward, but I wonder if it would be possible for you to provide me with a meal and a bed for the night. I haven't eaten decent food since leaving Sonora.'

'Dinner will be ready in about half an hour,' said Mary 'Are you a real preacher?'

'Preacher!' said the priest. 'Well now, I suppose some people would call me that but it isn't strictly true. I'm a priest, a Catholic priest. We don't call ourselves preachers. Does that bother you?'

'No,' said Mary, blushing. 'It's just that I've never met a Catholic priest before. I'll go see about dinner. Billy will explain.'

'I have that effect on some people,' said Father Ryan as Mary and Josh disappeared into the house. 'What is there to explain, Billy?'

Billy explained the circumstances and Father Ryan laughed, saying that he would be more than happy to perform the marriage ceremony. For some time he and Billy sat outside and Billy told him what had happened since they had last met. Father Ryan said that he was pleased Billy had seen sense and had not killed Fairfax, but he was somewhat thoughtful.

'Now that would explain why there was a man in Sonora who was asking about you,' he said eventually. 'He said something about wanting to arrange a fight with somebody, but it didn't really ring true. Anyhow, since nobody had seen or heard of you since you left, they couldn't tell him anything other than you were one hell of a fighter.'

'I'll bet it was one of Fairfax's men,' said Billy. 'Anyhow, Father, what brings you out this way? You're a long way from Sonora.'

'Ah well now,' said the priest with a dry laugh. 'I think I'm a good priest and I know I'm a good Catholic and I always do my duty to my parishioners and my bishop. One of the drawbacks with being a Catholic priest is that you can be moved to another parish whenever the bishop decides to move you. It always seems that he decides to move you just when you've found yourself a good little living and just when you've got to know everybody and all there is to know about a parish. I think they do it on purpose just so that you don't become complacent or become too used to the flesh pots. On the other hand I think they sometimes do it just to show who is in charge or to be just bloody minded. Whatever the reason, I've been moved to a town further north.'

'What happened to the idea of going back to Ireland and driving out the English?' asked Billy.

'Well now, that's another thing,' said the priest with a wry smile. 'Just about the time you were released from prison, my then bishop Matthew O'Connor — a good and loyal Irishman — died and was replaced by one Thomas Boulton. I never met Thomas Boulton but I have since discovered that he is an Englishman. Imagine that, an Englishman *and* a Roman Catholic! I never knew such animals existed and it still doesn't seem right. Anyway, there was no arguing about him being my bishop. For some reason only he knows, he decided to send me to a place called Gainsville. So, for the moment, my going back to Ireland is out of the question.'

'Father Ryan has agreed to wed us,' Billy announced as they were eating dinner. 'He says it doesn't matter about us not being Catholics. He says we're all the same in the eyes of God.'

'That's not quite what I said, Billy,' corrected the priest. 'I was careful not to include Englishmen in that.' He looked at both Mary and her father. 'You're not English by any chance, are you?'

'No,' said Josh. 'As a matter of fact I believe my grandfather and his wife were Welsh, wherever that is.'

'Wales,' said Father Ryan. 'Another nation oppressed by the English. That's all right then. When do you want me to perform the marriage?'

'As soon's you like,' said Billy. 'After dinner will do.'

'*Billy Nesbitt*!' scolded Mary. 'There are some things a girl likes to have some say-so in. I was hoping for a proper wedding, you know, in church with all my relatives and friends. *After dinner will do, indeed.* You make it sound like something I just took out of the cooking pot.'

'That's all very well, my girl,' said her father, 'but there's no church anywhere near here and I'm the only relative you've got.'

Mary suddenly smiled. 'Well, a girl can dream, can't she?'

The ceremony was performed after the meal, although Mary insisted that both men smarten themselves up while she put on her best dress. Just before the ceremony, Josh surprised everyone when he suddenly produced a gold wedding ring.

'It was your mother's,' he told Mary. 'I didn't give it you before, I didn't think much of that man you married. I was right too, even if he did kill himself. That was just about the only decent thing he ever did do.'

'Thanks, Dad,' she said, tearfully, giving him a kiss. 'And thanks, Mom.'

# 10

Two days after Father Ryan had left, Billy had to go to a trading post to collect stores previously ordered to see them through the forthcoming winter. He took the buckboard pulled by their working horse. As yet he had still not learned to ride a horse properly but he had learned to drive the buckboard. The trading post was a good six-hour ride away and when he eventually reached it, there was rather more excitement and activity than he might have expected.

There were several homesteaders also collecting stores and for some strange reason, Billy thought, they all seemed to be wary of him. He soon discovered the reason for the added excitement was due to a battered and bruised body having been brought in that morning. He also quickly discovered that the injured man was Father Sean Ryan. Most folk were quite surprised that Billy and Father Ryan should know each other. This only served to make them even more wary of him.

'Fairfax!' said the priest through a swollen lip. 'I ran into him yesterday. He knows you're somewhere around. I didn't tell him anything though. He didn't believe me because I said I'd come from Sonora. I had to admit I knew you, but I said that I hadn't seen you since Sonora. He tried beating it out of me.'

'I suppose it was only a matter of time before he showed up,' sighed Billy. 'Where is he now?'

'Could be anywhere,' said the priest. 'All I know is he was searching every homestead for you. He's been to most of these folk. How many people know where you live?'

'Don't know,' admitted Billy. 'I sure ain't made no secret of it.' He looked at the others. 'How many of you know me an' where I live?' he asked. They all shook their heads. If they did know or even suspected, it was obvious that nobody wanted to become involved. 'Looks like nobody does,' continued Billy. 'I don't buy that. It's plain to me that you all guessed who I was.'

'Then I suggest you get back and get Mary and Josh out of there,' said the priest. 'He's got at least three men with him and they all look as though they might rape Mary just for the hell of it.'

'What about you?' asked Billy. 'You sure don't look fit enough to travel anywhere on your own.'

'I'll be all right,' assured the priest. 'I've got a couple of broken ribs and a broken arm, they'll mend. You just get back and take your family to safety.'

'He can stay here a couple of days, but no longer,' said the owner of the trading post. 'He's right about that feller Fairfax. He was through here two days ago. He was lookin' for some feller called Billy Nesbitt. That's you, isn't it? I heard there was some new man out at Josh's place but I didn't tell them a thing. I guess I was lucky, they must've believed me. Most of these other folk have also had a visit from Fairfax but I don't think they know anythin' about you.'

'Billy Nesbitt, that's me,' confirmed Billy. 'They might not've known before, but they sure do now. How many men did you see?' He asked the same question of everyone else and all confirmed what Father Ryan had said.

'Same as the priest,' replied owner. 'Three men plus Fairfax. I didn't know his name was Fairfax until the priest told me, but it's the same man right enough. He sure seemed to want you pretty bad, but I don't think he was anythin' to do with the law. What you do to him?'

'It'd take too long to explain,' said Billy. 'OK, I'll just collect the order an' get back. It's my fault they did this to him an' I don't want to cause you no more trouble. I seem to have caused more'n enough of that already. I'll take him back with me.' Father Ryan tried to

233

protest but Billy waved his hand dismissively. 'You ain't in no fit state to go anywhere or to look after yourself. You're comin' with me an' I won't take no for an answer. Will you folk be all right?'

'Nothin' we can't handle,' said the store owner. 'Us mountain folk are pretty hard an' we do have to deal with the occasional outlaw. So far it's them what've always come off worst. I don't reckon this Fairfax and his men will give us too much trouble.'

'James Fairfax ain't outlaw,' said Billy. 'He's the biggest landowner in Greenwood. I'm surprised you ain't heard of him. He's also just about the most pigheaded man I ever met an' I can assure you I've met my share of those. Are you sure you'll be all right, Father? It's a long way back to my place.'

'I'll be fine,' insisted Father Ryan. 'Don't you worry about me, you just make sure Mary and Josh are safe. Now, if we're going, go — you don't have much time.'

Six of the other customers seemed to become a little bolder and confirmed that they too had had a visit from Fairfax and, in all but one case, none of them even knew Billy existed until then. The one who did apparently now claimed that Josh had mentioned Billy some weeks earlier, when Billy was heading for Greenwood. He maintained that he had not said a thing to Fairfax. However, there was something about the way he protested his innocence which made Billy quite certain that he had, and recently.

Fearing the worst, Billy drove the buckboard as hard as he dared with the injured priest aboard and made good time. However, about five miles from home, as he was about to pass the farm of their nearest neighbour, a dishevelled figure forced him to stop. It was the son of the neighbour.

'Ma an' pa need help,' croaked the youth. 'They've been pretty badly beaten an' pa don't look too good.'

'Four men?' asked Billy. The youth nodded. 'It figures they'd come to you first. How bad are they?'

'I guess pa took the worst beatin',' said the youth. 'But apart from a few cuts ma don't seem too bad. They was lookin' for you, Mr Nesbitt. I had to tell 'em where you lived, I had to stop them doin' what they did. They said if I didn't tell 'em they was goin' to kill pa.'

'I understand, son,' assured Billy. 'I hope you also understand I have to get back. Those same men did this to Father Ryan an' they could be doin' the same thing or even worse to Mary an' Josh. I'll try an' get back to you if I can.'

He drove on, urging the horse faster than ever, something to which the animal was plainly not accustomed. Eventually, just as the light was fading, he came within sight of the farm. The place appeared very quiet, unnaturally so, and at Father Ryan's insistence, Billy left him under the shelter of a tree while he investigated.

At first he was surprised and very cautious; there was no sign of Fairfax or his men, in fact there was no sign of anyone. The only indication that anything was wrong was when Sam raced out of the house, barking furiously. The fact that Sam had run out told him that there was nobody around. Nevertheless, he entered the house with great caution, not knowing what to expect. He was not armed, his only protection was a long pitchfork he picked up on the way in and was more for self-assurance than actual protection.

A scene of utter devastation greeted him. Broken furniture and crockery, the fire doused by having the contents of the cooking pot and a pot of hot water turned over on to it and at first there was no sign of Mary or Josh. Sam, who had followed him into the house, yapped and scrabbled at a pile of bedding and clothing on the floor. Billy heard a groan.

'Josh!' he gasped as he moved the bedding. 'Where's Mary?'

'Took her!' groaned Josh. 'Just burst in, took Mary, wrecked the place, beat me an' said to tell you she'd die unless you did what they wanted. Said they'd be back. Don't ask me how, but they somehow found out you lived here now.'

'I know how they found out,' said Billy. 'Which way did they go?'

'I don't know,' croaked Josh.

'Did they hurt Mary?'

'Not that I could see,' said Josh. 'Sam did his best to save her an' I thought they'd shot him. I heard a couple of shots an' he yelped.' He stroked Sam's head. 'Nice to see you're still alive, old feller.'

'It'd take more'n them to get rid of Sam,' said Billy. 'I reckon he can hear bullets comin'. I reckon he did get nicked though, there's a scratch on his rump, probably a bullet. How long ago was this?'

'Maybe two hours after you left this morning',' said Josh. 'I must've been unconscious since then.'

'They seem to have given you a pretty good beatin',' said Billy. 'Will you be all right?'

'I guess so,' said Josh. 'Just a few cuts an' bruises, no broken bones. You ain't goin' out there this time of night, are you? You'll never find 'em. You don't know the country round here. How're you goin' to be able to follow?'

'I got me a dog what can follow a particular fish through water,' said Billy. 'At least they won't see me comin'. Don't worry, I won't do nothin' stupid, not while they have Mary.'

'I'm comin' with you,' Josh tried to insist.

'No you ain't,' asserted Billy. 'I've got another job for you. I've got Father Ryan not far away. He's hurt pretty bad. He reckons he's got a couple of broken ribs an' a busted arm. I need you to look after him.'

'Father Ryan!' exclaimed Josh. 'Don't tell me, Fairfax got to him as well. Did he tell him where you were? I'd be surprised if he did no matter what they

239

did to him. He'd die first.'

'No, it wasn't Father Ryan,' assured Billy. 'Who it was don't matter, what does matter is findin' where they are an' gettin' Mary back. I'll go fetch Father Ryan. If you're up to it you can do a bit of tidyin' up an' get a fire started.'

Half an hour later, with Father Ryan in a bed and Josh busily preparing something to eat, Billy announced that he was leaving to find Mary. He ate a piece of bread and cheese, put on his gun and found a rifle. He filled his pockets with ammunition and called Sam.

'You take care now,' ordered Father Ryan. 'May the Good Lord look after you, but I have this feeling that you can look after yourself.'

'Ain't you takin' the horse?' asked Josh.

'No need,' said Billy. 'I reckon they can't be too far away. Anyhow, our horse is dead beat an' the donkey is too slow. Sam'll soon find 'em.'

Sam needed no telling and almost immediately seemed to pick up the scent. By this time it was dark, although there was a crescent moon which gave some little light. Sam, of course, needed no light to follow their scent.

Purely because he was walking, Billy's progress was slow. Whilst it might have been fairly easy going on a horse, the rough ground and the darkness made walking something of a challenge. However, Billy was in no mood to admit defeat.

He estimated that they had been following the trail for more than two hours and Billy was beginning to wonder if Sam really was following the scent of the horses. Quite suddenly Sam stopped, growled softly and crouched, waiting for Billy to catch up with him. When he did, Sam still did not move but growled again. Billy patted the dog's head, crouched down beside him and stared into the blackness.

'I can't see nothin', Sam,' he

whispered. The answer was another low growl. 'I'll just have to take your word for it.'

For some time they both lay quietly, Sam obviously knowing where someone or something was and Billy having to guess. He was not helped by the fact that a large cloud had chosen that moment to cover what little moonlight there was. However, after what he guessed was about ten minutes, Billy thought he detected a movement directly ahead of him.

Having eventually located someone, he found it easier to focus and was quite certain that there was a figure about ten yards ahead of him. As far as he could make out, there was only one.

'Go find Mary,' Billy whispered in Sam's ear. 'I'll deal with whoever that is.'

Sam was suddenly lost in the darkness and after a short time Billy started to ease himself forward very slowly and very carefully. The last thing he wanted was to have to shoot whoever was in front, that would simply alert the others.

He estimated that he had almost completely closed the gap when the cloud suddenly cleared the moon. Even in the faint light Billy could see that he was no more than three or four feet away from a figure sitting against a rock. He froze, fully expecting to be seen, but luck appeared to be on his side. There came a gentle snort, the kind of snort made by somebody on the verge of sleep Now quite certain that the figure was alone, Billy moved quickly.

There was a very brief struggle and a choking sound as Billy's huge hands closed around the unfortunate man's neck. Fingers clawed at Billy's hands but suddenly stopped as the body went limp and a faint snap, felt rather than heard, broke the man's neck. Billy checked that the man was indeed dead, propped the body against the rock to make it look as though he was still at his post and looked around for signs of the others.

In the faint moonlight, he saw the definite outline of what appeared to be a gully or narrow entrance to a valley. There was a faint glow from what seemed to be a cave and, as he slowly moved closer, he heard a voice.

'I'd know that voice anywhere,' Billy said to himself. 'Jimmy Fairfax. Well done, Sam. Just don't let him know we're here yet.' In answer to this observation, Sam was suddenly at his side, his tail wagging. He knew it was wagging because it beat against his leg. 'Yeh, Sam, I know where she is too. Now all we got to do is get her out of there.'

Even though he was quite certain where Mary was, he felt it was still essential that he knew her exact location, as there might not be enough time to start looking for her in the dark. Somehow he had to either get the remaining men out of the cave or get himself in a position where he could deal with them.

There was not enough light for him to see properly but he decided to go to his right. He was joined by Sam. The first things, he discovered were their horses hobbled behind some fallen rocks. From there, he felt his way along the side of the gully until he was exactly opposite the cave. It proved to be not so much a cave as a deep overhang of rock.

The light of the fire showed Mary was towards the rear of the overhang with one man immediately alongside her. There were two figures sitting by the fire in front of Mary, both with their backs towards Billy. The man sitting alongside Mary suddenly stood up, took a billycan from the fire and poured himself a mug of coffee. He offered some to Mary who apparently refused. He then exchanged words with the other two men, slowly drank his coffee and then came out of the cave. He stood and called out.

'Ted,' he called, 'Mr Fairfax says you can come in now, it's gettin' too cold out there.' Of course there was no reply from Ted. 'You hear me, Ted?' the man called again. 'You can come in now.' Again, no response. 'I reckon he's dropped off to sleep,' the man called back into the cave. 'I've half a mind to leave him out there an' let him freeze to death.'

However, it seemed James Fairfax did not go along with the idea of Ted having gone to sleep. He suddenly leapt to his feet, drew his pistol and picked up his rifle. On seeing this, the other man did the same.

'Maybe he has gone to sleep, maybe he hasn't,' said Fairfax. 'On the other hand maybe Nesbitt got to him first.'

'Nesbitt could never've followed us out here, not in the dark,' protested the man. 'I reckon he's gone to sleep. Ted's like that, he can fall asleep anywhere and at any time.'

'I only hope you're right,' muttered Fairfax. 'Get out there and make certain. Nesbitt might not be too bright in many ways, but he's no fool. If anybody can follow us out here, he can. Both of you get out there, find Ted and take a good look around. If you see so much as a shadow, you shoot at it. I'll keep an eye on the woman. He won't do anything to harm her.'

One of the men came straight towards Billy, almost as if he had seen him, although it was plain that he had not. He seemed to be heading for the horses. Billy quickly but quietly also made for the horses. He waited behind a large rock for the man to appear.

Almost unexpectedly the man was directly in front of Billy and no more than five feet away. The first and last sighting he had of Billy was when Billy swung his rifle butt directly at his head. The only sound was a dull thud and slight crunch as the man's skull gave way and he dropped to the ground. Billy made his way back to opposite the entrance.

For a few minutes there was total silence which was suddenly broken as the man looking for Ted called out.

'Ted's dead!' he called. 'You were right, Mr Fairfax, Nesbitt's around here somewhere.'

'I caught him sleepin' on the job,' Billy called out, unable to resist letting Fairfax know that he was there. 'Your other friend won't be comin' back either,' he continued. 'He's got a mighty sore head. He probably can't feel nothin' though.'

'Nesbitt!' called Fairfax. 'I should've known. OK, so you might've killed them two, but remember I've still got your woman here. I could kill her right now.'

'But you won't, Jimmy,' said Billy. 'You won't 'cos the moment you do, you are a dead man an' you know it. The only chance you've got of stayin' alive yourself is to make sure she stays alive. I can see you, Jimmy, but you can't see me. Oh, an' you out there,' he called to the other man. 'Don't get no ideas about sneakin' up on me. I got me a pair of eyes what can see anythin' in the dark.' He patted Sam's head. 'Are you all right, Mary? Have they hurt you?'

'I'm fine,' replied Mary. 'Just don't go doing anything stupid like getting yourself killed. That wouldn't do either of us any good.'

'I don't intend to,' said Billy. 'OK, Jimmy, rememberin' that I can see you but you can't see me, the next move is up to you. I ain't out to kill you, there's been enough of that. I will if I have to though. All I want is for you to forget all about me an' give me back my wife. Yes, Jimmy, she is my wife. That priest you beat up on married us.'

'You'll have me crying!' called Fairfax.

Sam, who had been standing with Billy, suddenly growled. Billy slipped the shotgun out of its holster, knowing that the growl meant that somebody or something was close by. Sam growled again and this time it sounded more urgent. Billy stepped back against the rock face of the gully and pointed the gun in the direction the dog appeared

249

to be indicating. He waited a few moments until he thought he detected a slight movement.

Another gun suddenly fired and was obviously very close, possibly too close as the bullet seemed to ricochet off the rock close to Billy's head. He could not help but let out a surprised grunt, but he did not shoot. The grunt must have been heard by the man who fired the shot.

'I think I got him!' came the cry. Billy now knew exactly where the man was.

'Sorry to disappoint you,' said Billy as he squeezed the trigger to discharge one of his deadly barrels. There was a cry of agony and Billy knew he had hit the man. At that distance and with the spread effect of the shot, it would have been very difficult not to hit him. Whether or not he was dead was unimportant at that moment. 'Seems like it's just you an' me now, Jimmy,' he called.

'You, me and her,' called Fairfax.

'Let her go an' you have my word

that I won't try to kill you,' said Billy. 'But if you so much as hurt one hair on her head I swear you'll be a dead man. The choice is yours, Jimmy. My way you get to stay alive, your way you get to die.'

Billy could see Fairfax clearly and had he been anything like really capable of using his rifle, killing him from that distance would have been easy. However, Fairfax had pulled Mary close to him and was obviously using her as protection. Given Billy's lack of ability, he knew that using either of his guns was totally out of the question. Fairfax remained silent for a few moments, apparently considering his options.

'OK, Nesbitt.' he said eventually. 'The one thing that could always be said about you was that you were always too dim to be anything but honest. I'm going to take a risk on you. I'm going to take her and my saddle over to where the horses are. I'm going to saddle my horse and then ride out. You'll know exactly where I am but I won't know where you are, so I certainly won't be taking any chances. You let me saddle my horse and then she goes free.'

'That's fine by me,' said Billy. 'Maybe you should ask Mary what she thinks about it. It is her life what's on the line, not mine.'

'I'll do whatever you think best, Billy,' she called out.

'Then I agree to what you suggest,' said Billy. 'Just remember though, Jimmy. I'll be in range with this cannon of mine an' you know from first hand what damage it can do.'

'You have a deal, Nesbitt,' said Fairfax.

Fairfax pushed Mary in front of him, picked up his saddle and prodded her in the back with his rifle. They both moved out into the blackness and for a few moments Billy totally lost sight of them. He moved towards where the horses were, almost tripped over the body of the third man on the way, and reached the horses at the same time as

252

Fairfax. It seemed thatFairfax could not see him.

The horse was saddled and even Mary helped. Fairfax quickly mounted, for a moment highlighted against the crescent moon. For a split second Billy was tempted to shoot. He had the man in his sights and even if he had used a rifle, he doubted if he could have missed.

James Fairfax had been right about one thing though: he, Billy Nesbitt, had given his word. Suddenly both horse and James Fairfax were gone. Billy rushed forward and embraced Mary.

'Let's get you back home,' he said. 'There's two injured men who need your help — Josh an' Father Ryan.'

'Father Ryan!' she exclaimed. 'What happened to him?'

'I'll explain as we go,' said Billy.

'There's three horses here,' said Mary. 'We could ride back.'

'Mary,' said Billy with a dry laugh, 'you sure picked one hell of a time to teach me how to ride. No, we'll walk.

Sam knows the way back, I know I sure don't. How about you? You ought to, you've lived in these parts all your life.'

'Not in the dark,' she had to admit. 'OK, but when it's daylight we come back here and collect these horses. They're too valuable to just leave out here.'

'It's a deal,' agreed Billy. 'Just don't expect me to learn to ride now. I'm bad enough when I can see what I'm doin'. What I'll be like if I can't see the horse an' the horse can't see me is anybody's guess. They'll be fine out here until we can get back for 'em. They're hobbled.'

When they eventually reached home, Billy was really surprised at just how much work Josh had been doing. Apparently even Father Ryan had insisted on doing something. There was still a lot to be done to get things exactly how Mary wanted them, but she seemed to appreciate the effort put in. It was not long before all four took to their beds and were soundly asleep.

It was daylight, but only just and

both Billy and Mary were awakened by Sam, who was in the barn, barking. Both of them knew enough not to ignore the dog. Billy grabbed his shotgun, told Mary to remain where she was and slipped outside.

At first there was nothing to be seen, but Sam was suddenly at his feet and very agitated. He raced off behind the barn where he barked furiously. At least Billy now knew where the intruder was. He also knew *who* the intruder was.

'Can't you ever give up, Jimmy?' shouted Billy. 'I know where you are.'

'I know what folk always used to say about me, Nesbitt,' came the reply. 'They always said I was pigheaded and for once I agree with them. It's between you and me, Nesbitt. I'm not interested in what happens to the others, all I want is you. Just you and me, out in the open, face to face. You said you could use a rifle, Nesbitt, let's see just how good you are.'

For one of the few times in his life Billy regretted boasting about his ability with a rifle, but it had been made in an attempt to frighten Fairfax. However, he too had a stubborn streak and was not prepared to admit that his ability was very limited.

'OK, Jimmy,' he called. 'Just you and me with rifles or handguns, I don't care which. I'll go get my rifle. You stay where you are, behind the barn.'

'You don't stand a chance!' protested Mary who had heard what had been said. 'You can't use either.'

'So what do you expect me to do?' he asked. 'I can't be lookin' over my shoulder for the rest of my life. He won't let it go so this thing has to be settled once and for all. Who knows, maybe I'll get lucky again.'

Josh and Father Ryan had also appeared, but neither made any attempt to talk Billy out of the challenge. Billy picked up the rifle, checked that it was fully loaded and went outside, ignoring Mary's protests.

He took a wide detour round to the back of the barn just in case Fairfax should try to kill him before they faced each other. Eventually he and Fairfax were facing each other. Billy was grim-faced, fearing the worst while Fairfax was almost laughing.

'I didn't think you'd have the guts to face me,' said Fairfax. 'I know you're not a coward, but I also know you can't handle a gun. I hope you said farewell to that new wife of yours.'

'Let's just get on with it,' grated Billy. By that time Mary and Josh had arrived, Mary clinging to her father. 'Your move, I think, Jimmy.'

James Fairfax did move as he drew his pistol. There was a single shot and Fairfax suddenly lurched forward, his pistol slowly dropped from his hand and a surprised look appeared on his face. Billy turned slightly to see Father Ryan holding a rifle, supported in the crook of his broken arm. It plainly hurt.

'I hope you don't mind, my boy,' said the priest. 'But being something of a gambling man, as you well know, I was thinking that the odds were not really in your favour. Everybody likes long odds when they win, but that's something that doesn't happen too often. Oh, and don't give me any of that rigmarole about priests not killing anybody. We certainly don't make a habit of it but sometimes extreme measures are needed even by us. Anyway, Fairfax was an Englishman and the only good Englishman is a dead one.'

'Thanks, Father,' said Billy. 'I'm grateful and you're probably right in thinking he would have killed me. The only trouble is, we'll never know if I could have done it or not.'

'That is a very selfish attitude to take,' scolded the priest. 'If it had just been yourself, I would have let things take their course. You're a married man now, Billy Nesbitt, you have a wife to think about.'

'I guess you're right,' sighed Billy.

In spite of the fact that James Fairfax had been prepared to kill him, Billy insisted that he be given a proper burial. Father Sean Ryan reluctantly agreed to perform the ceremony, making it quite plain that in his opinion the only suitable place for a dead Englishman was in the flames of eternal damnation.

A couple of days later they were all sitting at the table when Father Ryan looked Billy firmly in the eye.

'I know I said that you had responsibilities now, Billy,' he said, 'and to be sure, you have. I know from experience that earning money off the land can be very hard, so I got to thinking . . . '

'*No, Father!*' said Mary, very firmly.

'*No, Father!*' repeated the priest. 'Will you not have the grace to hear me out, woman? Billy is the man of the house now, he must decide.'

'If she says no, then no it is,' said Billy.

'Now don't be too hasty, young Billy,' continued the priest. 'After I left you before, I heard about a man called *The Bear*. He's a fist fighter about a hundred miles west of here and there's two hundred dollars to the man who can beat him. I want no part of that money, that would be all yours. I could make enough . . . '

'*No, Father!*' shouted Mary, Josh and Billy in unison.

## THE END

We do hope that you have enjoyed reading this large print book.

Did you know that all of our titles are available for purchase?

We publish a wide range of high quality large print books including:
**Romances, Mysteries, Classics**
**General Fiction**
**Non Fiction and Westerns**

Special interest titles available in large print are:
**The Little Oxford Dictionary**
**Music Book, Song Book**
**Hymn Book, Service Book**

Also available from us courtesy of Oxford University Press:
**Young Readers' Dictionary**
**(large print edition)**
**Young Readers' Thesaurus**
**(large print edition)**

For further information or a free brochure, please contact us at:
**Ulverscroft Large Print Books Ltd.,**
**The Green, Bradgate Road, Anstey,**
**Leicester, LE7 7FU, England.**
**Tel:** (00 44) **0116 236 4325**
**Fax:** (00 44) **0116 234 0205**

*Other titles in the*
*Linford Western Library:*

## STONE MOUNTAIN

### Concho Bradley

The stage robbery had been accomplished by an old woman. Twine Fourch had never heard of a female being a highway robber before. He followed the trail all the way to a dilapidated log cabin up Stone Mountain. What happened after that no one could believe even after townsmen from Jefferson found the old log house and the skeletal dying old woman. But before the mystery could be solved there would be two unnecessary killings, a bizarre suicide and a lynching.

# GUNS OF THE GAMBLER

## M. Duggan

Destitute gambler Ben Crow arrives in Mallory keen to claim his inheritance, only to discover that rancher Edward Bacon has other ideas. Set up by Miss Dorothy, who had fooled him completely, Ben finds himself dangling on the end of a rope. Saved from death, Ben sets off in pursuit of Miss Dorothy, determined upon retribution. However, his quest for vengeance turns into a rescue mission when she is kidnapped by a crazy man-burning bandit.

# SIDEWINDER

## John Dyson

All Flynn wants is to be Marshal of Tucson, but he is framed by the territory's richest rancher, Frank Buchanan, and thrown into Yuma prison. Five years later Flynn comes out, intent on clearing his name and burning for vengeance. Fists thud, knives flash and bullets fly as he rides both sides of the law and participates in kidnapping and double-dealing. He is once again arrested for a murder of which he is innocent. Can he escape the noose a second time?

# THE BLOODING OF JETHRO

## Frank Fields

When Jethro Smith's family is murdered by outlaws, vengeance is the one thing on his mind. He meets the brother of one of the murderers, who attempts to exploit Jethro's grudge in the pursuit of his own vendetta. The local preacher, formerly a sheriff, teaches Jethro how to use a gun. With his new-found skills, Jethro and his somewhat unwelcome friend pit themselves against seemingly impossible odds. Whatever the outcome lead would surely fly.

# SEVEN HELLS AND A SIXGUN

## Jack Greer

Jim Cayman had been warned about Daphne Rankin, his boss's wife, and her little ways. When Daphne made a play for Jim and he resisted, the result was painful and about what he had feared. But suddenly matters went beyond the expected and he found himself left to die an awful death. Only then did he realise that there was far more than a woman scorned. He vowed that if he could escape from the hell-hole he would surely solve the mystery — and settle some scores.